FALSE

U. E. Wynn

FALSE

Cover designed by Dynasty's Cover Me Book Covers
www.dynastyscoverme.com

ISBN-13: 978-1-7320325-1-4
ISBN-10: 1732032514

DEDICATION

This book goes out to my Uncles; Shawn Wynn, Mike Wynn and Jimmy Wynn. My grandfather, James Wynn, may you rest easy O.G. My great grandfather Eddie Enoch, rest easy commander in chief. Thank you for molding my character and laying the foundation for my morals and principles. I will forever be grateful to each and every one of you and I shall not let you guys down!

U.E. Wynn
.

ABOUT THE AUTHOR

U.E. Wynn

A self-educated, business savvy, humble entrepreneur was counted out at a young age by his peers, teachers, and family members. After enduring life altering events that would destroy and/or diminish any individual, he chose to overcome and excel. He turned what would be deemed a negative into a positive. He reevaluated himself and reclaimed a positive position within society.

U.E. Wynn is the founder of 501C nonprofit, Save a H.O.M.I.E. Inc. and an active activist within the community. He continues to assist disenfranchised youth, feed and clothe the homeless and bring forth literacy to the illiterate. Wynn also helps in providing a positive, productive and social atmosphere for the youth to unwind and enjoy themselves throughout the Carolinas via events, concerts and parties.

This is Wynn's second novel presenting you with a page turning, nail biting, exotic read.

PROLOGUE

There was a severe storm warning for the Tristate area and Matthew Baker left his job a little early to get home to his wife and children. The cold winter night air flowed like an arctic blast coming through the city as he stepped from the building. Looking around, he saw how quickly the snow was beginning to pile up.

"Shit," he cursed, digging his Timberland clad feet into a fresh bed of snow.

The snow was falling harder than it was a few hours ago and all he wanted to do was get home to his family. He shuffled to his car as fast as the snow allowed and shoved the key into the door. He practically dove into the car feeling the biting cold work through his coat. After starting the car, he sat there shivering letting the engine warm up a bit.

Waiting only about five minutes, Matthew was ready to start the twenty minute ride across town. He was bone tired after completing a double shift at work. The only thing that he wanted to do was get home, eat really quick, shower, and then curl up under the covers for the next two days. He was looking forward to the much needed rest and quality time he was going to spend with his two boys on his days off.

The music from the car's speakers played Keith Sweat's *"Make it Last Forever"* during the stations quiet storm mix. Humming the words of the song, Matthew came to a stop at the red light. He was only three to five minutes from the house and he was anxious to get there. The light turned green and he pressed the accelerator to go, but when he did, the front tires locked and spun out from the snow and black ice. The locking of the tires simultaneously with the acceleration of the gas, caused the car to lurch forward and spin out of control.

Gripping the steering wheel with both hands, Matthew braced

himself as he tried to gain control of the car. He jerked the car left, then right, panicking from the confusing turning.

"Fuck!" he shouted as the car spun around repeatedly heading in the direction of a pole. Pressing down on the brake seemed to make the car move faster and slide even closer to the pole.

Realizing that he was about to have a head on collision, Matthew reached for the driver's side door handle to open the door. He opened the door, but was unable to roll out because he was confined by the seat belt. Trying to unsnap the belt from his body quickly, the car hit the pole, and the belt tightened up across his chest and neck. Because the strap was so tight he was unable to breathe and the front end of the car was crushed pinning his legs beneath the dash.

Mathew's breathing became shallow and faint. He struggled with the strap around his neck, but it only got tighter. Being cut off from air caused a tear to roll down his face. Knowing that he wasn't going to be able to escape his certain fate, Matthew closed his eyes and allowed flashes of memories to flood his thoughts. He saw visions of his wife Gloria, and his two boys, Malik and Brandon. He was able to smile as he saw the birth of his son's, his wedding day, and all the many wonderful things that made him whole.

As he reminisced, he could hear in the background the sirens coming in his direction. However, help was going to be too late today. Opening his eyes, he saw the end looming in front of him as the pole, already wobbly from the crash, came down on the windshield. The force of the pole caused the top of the car's hood to collapse on his head. Less than minutes from his home and family, Matthew's life was extinguished. He would not be returning home ever again.

~~~~

Around two in the morning, a pounding knock jolted Gloria from her sleep. She rolled over to tap Matthew, but he wasn't there. With a twisted frown, she sat up in bed and drew a silk robe around her body. She walked over to the window to peek outside when she saw the flashing red and blue lights.

"Why in the hell are the cops at my door? And where is Matthew?" she asked aloud, shuffling down the hall.

Gloria whipped the door open and stared at the officers for a few moments.

"May I help you?" she asked, drawing her robe tighter around her body to ward off the chill.

"Sorry to bother you, Ma'am, but are you Gloria Baker?" the officer asked.

She looked from one officer to the other. Something was eerily amiss. *Where is Matthew*, she wondered, hesitating to respond.

"Yes… I'm Gloria Baker," she said and nervously swallowed.

"Ma'am, I'm sorry to inform you that your husband was in a car accident and…"

"Oh no," Gloria screeched. "Is he alright? What hospital is he in?" Her left hand shot up to her mouth and her eyes widened in fear.

"I'm sorry, Miss, but your husband didn't make it."

All of Gloria's worst nightmares became a reality. She sank to her knees while tears drenched her face. The officers tried to console her as she screamed her husband's name. Her knees buckled and the officer dropped down to the floor with her.

His mother's wailing woke Malik from his sleep. He quickly ran down the steps and saw the two officers in the doorway, the cold air freezing the foyer of their home.

"Ma?" he called out, confused when he saw her kneeled down on the floor crying. "Ma, what's going on?" he asked.

"Matthew!" she continued to cry. "Why?" Her sobs were uncontrollable, her words barely coherent.

"Where's Daddy, Ma? Please, tell me what's going on?" Malik walked over and got to his knees beside her. He pulled her from the officer and wrapped his arms around his mother.

She clung to his chest and cried harder. Malik had a hard time understanding what was happening, so he just rocked his mother back and forth. The officers presented their regrets once more and closed the door, leaving the two of them there alone. Since it wasn't a homicide, there was no reason for them to stay.

Soon, Malik was crying, too. He didn't know why, but to watch his mother fall apart made his heart hurt. Finally, she regained her composure and looked her oldest son in the eyes. She wiped her eyes and stood up.

"Go and get your brother," she whispered.

"What happened to Daddy?' Malik asked, but she walked away heading towards the kitchen.

Malik did as he was told. Wiping his tears, he went to wake up his brother, Brandon. He placed his hand on his shoulder as they went into the kitchen where their mother was sitting at the table. Her robe was hanging off of her shoulder and her eyes were bloodshot red.

"Sit down," she ordered softly.

The boys looked at one another as they took seats across from their mother. She stared down at her trembling hands and played with the edges of the placemat in front of her. She swallowed hard and then cleared her throat. Looking up at her sons, her heart was pounding. How was she going to tell them that their father was dead? How was she going to tell them that they would have to live the rest of their life without him? She took a deep breath and tried to speak.

"Boys, your father..." Her words were swallowed with tears and agonizing sobs.

"He's dead, isn't he?" Brandon asked.

She looked at him through her tears and slowly nodded her head. Brandon's eyes sweltered with anguish. His fists balled into tight knots and his chest heaved up and down. His father was dead. He will never see him win the Science Fair Award or teach him how to catch like he'd shown Malik. *He promised to teach me how to catch too. How could he have broken his promise?*

Malik hugged his little brother, trying to comfort him as his own emotions surfaced. He would have to learn to be a man without the one person he admired the most. *How can I be a good man like him if he's not here to show me?*

The family sat there, huddled together with nothing but their sobs filling the quiet room. They were all equally heartbroken over the death of Matthew Baker, and their family would never be the same afterwards.

Two weeks later...

The casket was closed and covered with a beautiful floral arrangement. A few pictures of Matthew had been blown up and were scattered around the pew. Gloria thought it would be best to have a closed casket because Matthew didn't look like himself when she went to identify his body. The car had caught fire and the majority of his bottom torso had been burned. Not to mention the pole that came down on top of the car had crushed the left side of his body.

She and their two boys sat in the front row at the small church they attended weekly led by Pastor Daniels. Most of the people there were from their congregation and the rest were family and friends. Brandon laid his head in her lap blankly staring forward while Malik sat close with his arms wrapped securely around her shoulder. Gloria dried her eyes with a handkerchief and stood when the Pastor called her name.

"God is Good," she said and lifted her bible towards the seated mourners.

"All the time," some of them responded.

"My husband," she started, a tear sliding down her cheek, "worked day in and day out to make sure that me and our kids were well taken care of. I don't know why the Lord saw fit to call him home so soon, but I do know that he was a man of his Word and that he is up there having a party with his Momma," she said and smiled softly.

"He was always the life of the party, with a big smile and a big heart. That's what I will remember and you should too. My sons and I will like to thank you all for coming from the highways and byways to help us say a final goodbye to Matthew and..."

"Goodbye!" Malik sprung to his feet. "I don't want to say goodbye to my father. Not yet, Ma!" He ran over to the casket and lay both of his hands down on top of the black lacquer casket. His young shoulders shaking from the force of holding in his sobs. "This ain't fair! I want my father back!" Malik yelled with such force that most of the people broke down and began to cry. The anguish in his voice touching their very souls.

Gloria stepped down and rushed to his side. It was the first time Malik had really showed grievances since the night she told them about Matthew's death. He was trying to be strong for his mother and brother, but his heart was in pain. He squeezed his lips tightly while clenching his teeth as he sobbed. His tears dropped onto the flowers and left dark, wet stains on his suit.

"I'm never going to see my father again," he whispered hoarsely.

"Oh, my baby," whispered Gloria softly, holding him to her bosom.

A few family members went over to assist them back to their seats. They took a moment to get themselves together so the service could continue. A few minutes went by, and soon Brandon and Malik were watching quietly as they loaded the casket into the back of the hearse. Gloria and the boys got into the limo and Mathew's money hungry sisters and brothers climbed in with them. Gloria slid a pair of shades onto her face and stared out of the window for most of the ride.

"Well, Gloria," Mathew's eldest sister Sheryl started first. "I know you got a nice piece of change."

Gloria didn't say anything out of fear that this would become a double funeral. She didn't care that her sister in law was right about the money. There was a one-hundred-thousand-dollar life insurance policy in place for Matthew. It was enough to pay off some bills and ensure that they lived comfortably for a while. Gloria hadn't worked since they were married and that's how Matthew wanted it. He allowed her to live a lifestyle that she was going to miss. But one thing was for certain, his family would never get any of the money from his insurance policy.

"I know she hears me talking to her," Sheryl said to their brother Barry. "She always acted like she was better than us anyway."

"Leave my Momma alone," Brandon interjected.

His aunt cut her eyes at him. "Stay in a child's before I..."

"Now, watch it," said Gloria, pulling the shades from her face. "Don't say anything to my sons. You got that?"

No one said a word seeing how Gloria's whole body was tense and she looked like she meant business. Since nothing else was said, Gloria calmed herself and placed her hand in Brandon's. Soon, the car came to a slow stop and the driver stepped out and opened the door for them.

She watched as everyone began climbing from their cars making their way over to the plot that would be Matthew's final resting place. A light mist began to fall looking like a cloak of tears surrounding them. With Malik and Brandon by her side, Gloria walked that long walk across the soggy grass to say goodbye to her husband, lover and friend.

Standing in the front of the grieving guests, the Baker family was there paying their respects. Gloria rocked from side to side while holding Brandon, who sobbed uncontrollable. Malik, the now appointed man of the house, sat there with a face of stone. All he could think about was how he had to fill his father's shoes and make sure that his family would be alright. In his mind, he knew he would honor his father by being the rock his mother and brother needed.

Everyone's attention fell on the woman that made her way to

stand by the Pastor. Their solemn faces watched as she lifted her head and began to sing. Her voice was strong and comforting as she bellowed out the words to *Amazing Grace*. The words of the song touched everyone, and the mist coming down only solidified that a good man was going to meet his judgment on the other side.

It was now time to leave Matthew to rest in peace. The funeral director signaled to the people that the burial was about to commence. Throughout the crowd silent cries could be heard and people began to make their way back to their vehicles. Now, all but Gloria and her sons remained. The three of them stood in unison and walked to the edge of the plot and watched as the ditch-diggers began their job.

As each man dug their shovel into the ground and brought up dirt, they threw it on the casket as it descended six feet into the earth. Gloria threw her white rose on top of the casket as a trail of tears fell slowly down her face. Grabbing his mother's hand, Brandon looked up at her and held her gaze. They were lost for words, so they simply embraced and shared their sorrow together.

Malik looked to his right and saw his mother and brother hugging, and his heart melted with the pain of losing his father, and hero. He stepped closer to the edge of the plot to have a private and brief conversation with his father. He breathed in deeply and released it slowly.

"Pops, I can never fill those size thirteen shoes of yours, but I'm going to try. I'm glad that we were able to have fifteen years here together. You took care of us, but now I've got us. I love you Pop and I'll be back soon so we can talk again."

After speaking his heart to his father, Malik was now ready to take his place as the man of the house. Standing straighter than before, and feeling as if his father was smiling down on him, he walked over to his mother and brother.

"It's time for us to go. He doesn't want us crying like this."

He grabbed his mother's hand and she grabbed Brandon's. The three of them walked away from the cemetery to face their new world, with Malik leading the way.

CHAPTER 1

Two Years Later…

"Malik!" Gloria yelled from the kitchen. "Malik!"

Malik shoved his notebook under his pillow and hopped from the bed. "Yes, Ma?"

"I'm about to leave for work. I left dinner in the oven. Make sure Brandon finishes his homework, you hear?" She looped her purse on her shoulder and looked around for her keys.

"Okay, Ma." Malik sighed.

"What's the matter with you?" She looked at him curiously.

Malik sat down at the table and looked down in his lap. "You've been working all these long hours and we still don't have a lot of money."

Gloria sat down next to him and lifted his chin to make him face her. "Look at me, boy."

Malik stared into his mother's soft brown eyes. He knew she was tired of changing old people's diapers and making sure they took their Meds. In the past few months she had taken on two new clients. She was never home. Either she was at work or asleep.

"I have this under control. Don't you start worrying about stuff that has nothing to do with you, you understand?"

"Yes, Ma'am."

She placed a quick kiss on his forehead and stood. Seeing her keys, she picked them up from under a magazine and stuffed them into her pocket.

"Don't forget to take out that trash too."

It wouldn't have mattered if Gloria had to work six jobs to make ends meet. She wanted the best for her boys. She never wanted them to know that she had to play 'Eeny, Meeny, Miney, Mo' to decide which bill to pay first. Sometimes they went without cable, but they were never hungry, and she was not going down to Welfare. That in itself was a job. Gloria was steadfast about the boys going to school and getting good grades. She wanted them to go to college and make something of themselves. It was what she and Mathew both wanted for them and she was determined to see it through.

That was too far off though to Malik. He watched his mother drag herself to work every day and he knew he had to do something. When they buried his father, he vowed to take care of his family and become the man of the house. The bills were piling up and the cabinets were becoming bare. There had to be a way he could help his mother.

It was times like these that the promise he'd made to his father would keep him up at night. The way he saw it, the only answer to helping his mother was to get a job. The more he thought about it the more determined he was to get a job to help support his family.

It took him days to finally get the courage to ask Gloria if he could get an after-school job.

"Nope," her back was still turned to him as she stirred a pot of greens. "You will focus on school and school only."

"But Ma, if I get a job I can buy my own clothes and help you pay…"

Gloria turned swiftly on her heels and pointed the hot spoon at him. "I've told you not to be worried about my responsibilities and I'm not going to tell you again. Now, you will not get a job. You will go to school; that's your job!" She stared at him hard before turning around and going back to stir the pot of collard greens.

Malik was all for his mother's vision until he realized that making money was more important, and *that* became his priority. Although he knew that graduating with his class was on his 'to-do' list, he wanted to show his mother that he could keep up his grades and have a job. So when he saw there was a 'Help Wanted' sign in the window of a small cleaning company a few blocks from his house, he rushed in.

"Mr. Johnson," Malik greeted the owner with a handshake. "My name's Malik Baker. I see that you need some help around here."

"Frankly," said the old man, "I do." He looked Malik up and down and was satisfied with what he saw. The young man was neatly dressed and groomed. He wasn't sagging his pants or wearing too tight jeans. He looked to be someone that would put forth a good impression of his business.

"Well, I'm looking for work," said Malik with a smile. *Please let this man give me this job,* he silently prayed.

"Now, I can't pay you much, but…"

"Sir, anything would do."

Mr. Johnson smiled. He could see that the young man was determined. "Well, then I guess I will see you tomorrow at four thirty. There will be a few forms to fill out, but the job is yours."

Yes! "Thank you, sir. I'll be here."

The next day, Malik hurried home and stuck around to make sure Brandon did his homework. It took longer than it needed to because he kept playing around. When he was finally done Malik hopped up ready to get going.

"Look, I have something I gotta do. Don't open the door for anyone. When I come back, I'll knock on the window to let you know it's me."

"Where are you going?" Brandon asked, looking worried.

"Don't worry about it." Malik tossed his backpack on the floor. "And don't tell Ma."

"It must be something you shouldn't be doing if you're telling me not to tell Ma," Brandon said flatly.

"Just for once keep your mouth shut, Damn. You're always acting like a baby."

"I don't act like a baby," he snapped in resentment.

"Well, babies tattle tale. Are you a snitch now?" Malik was trying to convince Brandon to keep his secret by calling him out as a baby. Ever since their father died, he's become whiny. He's also been telling every little thing that Malik did wrong just to see him get in trouble. Their mother said he was just going through a phase and would grow out of it. Malik hoped he would hurry up and get through it because although he loved his brother and would do anything for him, he was becoming annoying as hell.

"No! I'm not a snitch," Brandon said, lifting his head indignantly.

"Aight then. Keep your mouth shut and I'll be right back," Malik said, heading down the hall. "And remember, don't open this door until you hear me knock. You got that?"

Brandon nodded his head as Malik eased out of the front door.

Mr. Johnson was sitting at the front desk when he walked into the building. He briefly looked up from his paperwork and gestured for Malik to have a seat.

"Okay, I need you to take care of this here building down the street. It's a three story office building. All you will be doing is emptying the trash in the offices. Someone else will be doing the bathrooms. You will always be supervised by an adult on each floor. Think you could handle that kind of work," Mr. Johnson asked.

Malik nodded his head with a smile. "Yes, sir." He was willing to do whatever it took to help his mother with the mounting bills.

Mr. Johnson supplied everything he needed and gave him the address to the building. The job was easy and for a few weeks Malik cleaned that building from top to bottom with four other young guys around his age. He lived for the day when Mr. Johnson would give him a one hundred and fifty dollar check every Thursday afternoon. He wouldn't spend a dime either. He would cash it and take it home, then stuff it in one of the pockets of his winter coats hanging in his closet.

One night, Malik was jolted awake from a deep sleep. He hadn't been dreaming, or anything. Something just made him wake up. Needing to go to the bathroom, he left his room and walked quietly down the hall. As he was about to pass by the kitchen, he looked inside to see his mother sitting at the table with the bills and her checkbook in front of her. He quietly slid back into his room and closed the door. He pulled the money he'd collected from Mr. Johnson from his coat pocket and sat on his bed.

He started to count, "One, two, three, four hundred and fifty dollars? What the fuck?" he cursed under his breath.

He knew it wasn't nearly enough to help out with any of the big bills, but he still wanted to offer it to his mother. He eased out his room quietly with the money held tightly in his hand. Before he reached the kitchen, he heard his mother sniffle. She was sitting at the table crying, stressing and calculating how her check was going to cover the bills. Malik's eyes watered up, but he refused to let the tears fall. Instead, he became angry. Angry with himself for failing his father. For failing his family.

He turned around angrily and retreated to his bedroom. He closed the door and plopped down on the bed tossing the crumpled bills on the night stand. That was chump change compared to the money his father made. He couldn't present that to her. It would be embarrassing.

I have to find a way to help, he thought sullenly. *I won't give up. Dad wouldn't!*

Long after his mother had gone to bed, Malik walked out his room and over to the table where his mother had sat. He looked at the stack of bills and saw that a lot of them were past due, but the one that caught his eye was the one from the building's management office. The letter stated that they had forty-five days to come up with the current month, past due month, plus late fees, or they would have to evacuate the premises. They were on the verge of being evicted.

It wasn't enough that they had to move out of the house they lived in to move into this small apartment. But now to see that they couldn't even afford this small, cramped space made Malik angry. He was not about to sit back and allow his mother to struggle. He was the man of the house and it was time that he started acting like it.

I know she won't like it, but I gotta do what I gotta do, he whispered into the wee hours of the night.

~~~~

The next day, Malik got up and dressed for school. All day long all he could think about was the money they needed. The money he'd saved didn't even come close to what they needed. Even with the money he had left over from his father's life insurance policy that his mother had given him, would barely cover half.

He was so disgusted with himself that he decided he needed to do something drastic. Something that he knew his mother wasn't going to approve of. But, in his mind, desperate times called for desperate measures. When he came to the final conclusion about what he was about to embark on, he went home to add the $1,550 from his share of the life insurance money to the $450 from his job. This would be enough to start his climb in the underworld.

~~~~

Two days after witnessing his mother's financial breakdown at the table, Malik was out wandering around the neighborhood. The hood was filled with abandoned buildings, liquor stores and overstocked bodega's. All around him were alcoholics, drug users, dealers and kids playing. Although his mother had made sure he kept his head in his books, he was no stranger to the way things went down in the streets and he figured what he didn't know, he'd learn.

Malik was out combing the streets looking for a guy name Rashad that was known in the streets as a connect. He knew he couldn't just walk up to one of the dealers and ask for him, so he decided to walk around until he saw him. It was late in the afternoon when he finally saw him enter a corner store. Walking into the corner store right behind him, Malik made his move. He was standing in the aisle watching as he checked the shelves.

Not knowing how to proceed, Malik decided to dive right in head first. "I got two stacks. I need half of it on that Sour and the remainder on them Molly's."

Malik knew that he was taking a risk and there was always the possibility that he was about to be rejected, or worse beat down and robbed for his money. However, he was coming to him as a man and he hoped he and Rashad could handle business as such.

When the man continued to browse the isle, Malik got a little nervous. Not wanting his opportunity to pass him by, he took another approach.

"Look, I know this may not be the right place. So I'm gonna leave my number to my burner with your boy in the truck. Have him hit me when the shit's together and we can exchange cash for product."

After saying what he needed to say, Malik turned from Rashad and headed for the exit. On the outside, he saw the black on black Tahoe with tinted windows, double parked at the curb.

With the same confidence that he exhibited when he approached Rashad, Malik walked over and tapped on the window. The man on the inside turned and looked out at him with his face twisted in a snarl. To let the guy inside know that he was not there to do him any harm, Malik stepped back from the truck and stretched his arms out showing him that he was not carrying a weapon. The window came down half way and the barrel of a shotty was pointed directly at Malik's chest. Before there was a word spoken from the man inside the car, Rashad walked out the store and stood beside Malik.

He studied the boy before him carefully. After a few seconds of non-verbal communication, Rashad broke the muteness and tapped Malik on the arm, and nodded in the other direction. It was an indication that he wanted to talk with him. The two of them walked the few steps to the curb, but before they could talk, the dude from the truck walked swiftly to where they were.

The unwelcomed third wheel looked Malik up and down. "Yo,

Rashad, you cool? Let me know what's up, cause you know what I'm about," he said as he patted the front of his pants indicating that his gun was in hands reach.

"Nah, Vice. Everything's cool. I need to holla at Lil' Man. Wait for me in the truck tho," said Rashad to his *'day one homie.'*

Vice stared hard at Malik again, then nodded. "Aight," he said, backing away.

After Rashad saw that Vice was back inside the truck he turned his attention back to Malik. He took a sip from his twenty once Coke and placed the top back on the bottle.

"I like people with confidence," he said as he started walking again. Malik quickly fell in step beside him. "But what you did was reckless and stupid." He glanced over at Malik with a serious expression. "Don't do that shit again. You feel me?"

Malik nodded, but said nothing.

Seeing that Lil' Man had respect and kept his mouth shut, he kept talking. "So you trying to cop?"

"Yeah, just like the next nigga. I'm on that paper chase. But I ain't built for that corner shit. I'm a boss in the making," he told him without a hint of humor or fear.

Rashad took an instant liking to the young kid and had to laugh at his comment. He could see from the gate that the boy standing before him mindset was far more advanced than the little nigga's he had running his corners. The *block boys* were cool with making that change while the boy in his presence saw the bigger picture. This kid was all about making them dollars.

Rashad smiled. "I'll fucks with you Lil' Man. What's your name?"

"Malik."

"Aight, Malik. Put this number in your phone." Rashad called out his math. "Call the number tomorrow around three. A chick name Peaches is going to tell you where it's at. Leave my money and take yo shit. Don't be stupid or start thinking you can make an easy come up. That's how nigga's get wet, ya dig?"

Malik understood and nodded. "I feel you."

Rashad was about to walk away, then stopped. "Check this Lil' Man. If you trynna bring that heat my way or you working for them badges, I'll end you. You feel that?"

"I ain't here for all that action," said Malik calmly. "But, I hear you."

Rashad stared at him hard. "Aight," he said, taking another swallow of his soda. He scanned the block not seeing anything suspicious. He nodded. "Tomorrow." Done with what he needed to say, he started to walk back to his truck thinking that he might have found his protégé.

After locking the phone number in his phone, Malik started the five to six-minute walk to the Family Dollar store to buy another burner. He knew once he talked with the chick the next day that the phone he had was dead. After leaving the store, there was one more stop he needed to make before he headed home. Jumping on the subway, he headed across town, and within thirty minutes he was on the other side.

Walking from the subway terminal, he headed north in the direction of the cemetery. He needed to have a conversation with his Pops. The short walk from the terminal to the cemetery gave Malik a quick moment to think about what he was about to get into.

After entering the *Holy Memorial Cemetery*, Malik walked up the path and passed by scores of graves. He knew that he was getting closer to where he needed to be and felt his stomach tighten. Malik cut off the path and began looking at the headstones. He walked passed a few more graves before he was standing in front of a headstone that read Matthew Baker. Malik was silent as he looked at the headstone. He felt his eyes begin to well up with tears and they started to fall on his face.

The late afternoon breeze blew the tree leaves, and caused the uncut grass to sway. The sun was still high in the sky, but was setting slowly in the West. Malik stood at 6'1, and had the build of a young LL Cool J. His caramel skin was smooth and his dark brown eyes were bright with the hope of a prosperous future. The dimples that were deep in his cheeks made his white smile stunning and sexy. In conjunction with his smile, Malik's lips were soft and inviting. His physical attributes were an assemblage of sexy, thuggish and nerd, creating a tempting package.

Malik stood there for at least five minutes, allowing the tears to fall freely. This was the only place he would allow himself to show his pain over losing his father. Feeling ready to have his talk with his dad, he walked a few steps closer to the headstone and placed his hand on top of it. He looked upward to the heavens.

"What's up, Pop!" Breathing in slowly he closed his eyes, trying to get his words together to continue. He reached up and wiped the tears from his face.

"I miss you. I wish we could have had a little more time together. There was so much more you had to teach me and Brandon. But I'm thankful for the time we had with you though. Anyway, you know after you left, Mom's been holding us down."

"The money from the insurance kept us afloat up until about six months ago. Then shit started going downhill from there. The money was running out, but she didn't ask nobody for nothing. She began working double shifts to keep food on the table and a roof over our heads. We don't get to see her all the time, but Brandon and I understand the struggle."

"Being that I'm the man of the house now, I can't let our family struggle or allow Ma to work so hard. So I'm about to do something you won't like, but I'm hoping you'll understand. I decided to make my bed to feed our family. I needed to come and let you know what I'm about to do, and that I'm doing the best that I can. Don't be mad at me," he said with his head down, ashamed. He knew that being a drug dealer went against everything his father stood for. "I'm not doing this for me. It's for the family," he whispered softly.

Time went by with Malik just standing there with his head bowed and his eyes closed. Trying to cope with loss and the problems at home was hard, but he knew what he had to do. Lifting his head, Malik sighed heavily. "I got to get home. I love you, Pop."

Malik had made his confession to his father, and as he was about to turn and walk away when the flowers that were in a planter on the headstone a few feet away fell over. The planter broke and the flowers were scattered on the headstone and the ground. The sudden crash caused Malik to jump.

He took that as a sign from his father, but he was unsure if it was a good sign or a sign for the worse. Either way, he was now in a situation that he was not able to retract. Whatever the consequences were going to be, he was willing to accept them. Tomorrow when he called Peaches, his journey as a dope boy would begin.

CHAPTER 2

Malik walked in the house from school, smiling because he'd beaten his little brother Brandon home. As he walked in, he tossed his book bag down on the floor before calling out to see if his mother was at home.

"Yo, Ma! You home?" he shouted out. When there was no response, he knew he was alone. Hurrying, he grabbed his book bag, rushed to his bedroom, and closed the door behind him.

Malik opened his bag and pulled out several zip lock bags of weed and pills. He counted up what he had left and calculated what his profit was going to be. Getting up from his bed, he walked over to his closed closet door and opened it. The closet was beyond junkie. He had clothes, shoes, hats and other articles strewn around in a total mess. His closet was the only portion of his bedroom that was not clean. Malik usually was surprisingly very neat and tidy for a young man. However, the closet was purposely kept that way to keep his secret life in the streets hidden from his mother.

Dragging some things from the top of the pile and digging towards the back, Malik pulled out an empty Timberland boot shoe box. On the inside was several rolls of money tightly bound by rubber bands and a few bags of weed. He pulled the rolled money out and started counting it up. When he got to the last band he heard the front door opening. Quickly placing the money and drugs back in the box, Malik replaced it on the floor and covered it up. He was placing his clothes and other items back on top of his stash when Brandon walked to his bedroom door.

"What are you doing?" he questioned, trying to peer over Malik's shoulder.

Not expecting his brother to sneak up behind him, Malik hurried up and got up from the floor closing his closet door behind him. He turned and looked down at Brandon.

"Nothing. Why you in my room anyway without knocking? How many times I have to say that shit to you?"

"My bad. You didn't answer when I asked was anybody home. So I decided to see if you were in here. You don't have to get mad," he said in a deflated tone.

Seeing that his little brother was taking his words to heart, Malik wanted to dead the situation. He placed his arm around his brother's neck and pulled him in close for a side bear hug. Malik loved his brother and would do what he had to do to protect him and their mother. It would kill his spirit if Brandon found out anytime soon about what he was doing for money. He had been living a double life for weeks for his mother and brother, and he knew sooner or later, his secret life was going to be exposed.

The two of them walked out of the bedroom and into the kitchen. They laughed and joked around as Malik listened to Brandon tell him about his day at school and another award that he'd received for his grades. This was their ritual every day after school, with or without their mother being home.

After washing his hands, Malik started seasoning the thawed chicken that his mother had left in the sink for tonight's dinner. As he listened to what Brandon was saying, he was also thinking about the lie of living two lives that he was trying to keep hidden. *How the hell am I going to explain this to her.*

~~~~

Gloria was done with her shift for the evening and was glad to be headed home. She was even happier that she now had enough to pay the money she owed for the back rent and the current rent that was due. It had taken her damn near a month of double shifts and working seven days a week to get up the money, but she had gotten it. Gloria had spoken with the rental management company two weeks beforehand, and told them that she would have the payment in full today.

She'd gotten off from work with enough time to get from her last client's house to the rental office before it closed. This was the first time in a while that Gloria actually felt as if she had accomplished something. For the first year after Matthew's passing, she had been in a functional state of depression. Although she was still being a good mother and going to work, she was in a mental hell without her better half to lean on.

It wasn't until one night when she was in her bedroom crying her eyes out that she felt as if Matthew's spirit was surrounding her. His presence was so real to her that she knew she heard his voice whisper in her ear. *'Gloria, pull yourself together. Malik and Brandon need you.'* After that night she was no longer depressed, because she knew he was still by her side.

Turning the corner of Monterey Street, Gloria was less than five hundred feet from the rental office premises. Pulling her old car into the parking lot and grabbing her purse, she was there with ten minutes to spare before they were closed for the day. She stepped inside, smiling because paying her back rent would lift a huge burden from her shoulders. She looked inside her purse confirming that the five thousand dollars in money orders were still in the envelope.

Immediately, when the door chimed and Gloria entered, Debbie looked at her with a perplexed look on her face. She stood up to greet her with a smile of her own.

"Hello Ms. Baker. What brings you here this evening?"

With Debbie's greeting, Gloria sent the woman a look of confusion. She was absolutely positive that she'd called and advised her that she would be in the office with the money for the past due rent. She reached into her purse and pulled out the envelope.

"I'm here to pay my rent and the two months past due amount, plus the fees. I'm sure that we spoke last week about this." She was hoping that Debbie had just forgotten about their conversation.

After hearing the reason why Gloria was in her office, Debbie was now even more confused. Their back rent and their current due rent had been paid in full over a week ago. Her son Malik had come in with money orders totaling the five thousand and squared up what they owed.

He came in a few days after Gloria had called the office. Debbie was thinking that Malik was bringing the money they'd spoken about because Gloria wasn't able to bring it in the office herself. She reached down and picked up the clipboard that was lying on her desk.

"I'm sorry, but there must be some misunderstanding. According to my spreadsheet, you're paid in full until next month. Your son Malik came in with the money orders and paid last week."

Gloria wasn't sure if she'd heard correctly. How did her son even know about them being on the verge of getting evicted? Better yet, where did he get five thousand dollars to pay the rent?

"Debbie do you have a copy of the money order?" She needed to see it.

Debbie opened a folder that was also on her desk. She shuffled through a few papers until she found what she was looking for. She handed Gloria a copy of the five money orders.

Gloria looked at the money orders and examined the handwriting on it. She instantly recognized Malik's neat writing style. She handed the copies of the money orders back to Debbie. *Where did he get five thousand dollars?*

Debbie was standing behind her desk watching Gloria. When she smiled wanly at her, she watched as she shoved the envelope back into her purse.

"Thank you for your time Debbie," said Gloria and turned towards the door. She left in a hurry, rushing to get home so she could question Malik.

The ride home for Gloria was unbearable. There were so many thoughts going through her mind. There was so many questions and her fear was that she was not going to be able to handle the truth.

She made it home safely and carefully parked the car in front of their apartment. Turning the car off, she remained seated for a few minutes using the solitude to prepare for the conversation with her son. She took one final moment for herself before exiting the car and walking inside the building.

As she took the elevator to the third floor, the anticipation was causing her to sweat, and beads of moisture began to form on her forehead. Her heart began to beat a tad faster. Placing the key inside the door and turning the knob, Gloria was ready to hear the truth.

~~~~

As soon as he heard the door open then close, Brandon hopped up to greet his mother. Without giving it a second thought, he ran up to her and started blurting out the high points of his day at school. Gloria, who was so focused on getting to the bottom of how Malik got that money for the back rent, without meaning to, snapped at him. She barely even acknowledged Brandon as she said, "Not now," and proceeded to walk into the kitchen for some explanations from her oldest son.

Malik heard his mother yell at Brandon and her tone of voice made him look in her direction. Their mother rarely raised her voice, so when he heard her yell, he knew something was wrong. Stepping from the kitchen, he met his mother as she was coming in his direction. The two of them almost bumped heads as they were standing face to face and eye to eye. Not knowing what was wrong, Malik spoke first.

"Ma, what's wrong?"

Gloria studied her son's eyes. She no longer saw a young boy standing before her. For the first time, she saw him as a man. However, her eyes could also see that he was thinking of how to deal with whatever she was about to throw his way. She told herself that whatever lie he was concocting in his mind wasn't going to be accepted. She was holding the strap of her purse with her left hand, but her right hand was still free. Devoid of facial expression, she swiftly connected her open-handed right palm across Maliks' face.

The slap that connected to her son's cheek was powerful. The force alone, stunned him and made Malik stumble backward. Before he even had the opportunity to ask his mother what he had done, and why she was attacking him, she spoke in a tone that was so calm and collected that it came off sounding almost peaceful.

"I've been to the rental office. Where did you get the five thousand dollars to pay for the rent? You better think twice about lying to me before you answer," Gloria warned.

Malik looked at his mother and was thinking of the right way to inform her of his life choices. If he was going to be the man of this family, then he needed to come clean and tell his mother the deal. He already knew that no matter what she said, or how she felt, he wasn't going to stop. They needed the money and it was up to him to get it. Looking his mother in the eye, he was ready to confess his sins.

"Ma, let me explain. First of all, I'm the man of the house now, and it's my job to take care of my family the same way it was for Dad. He provided for us and now so will I. I promised him I would," he said with a hint of anguish in his voice. "I refuse to see my mother working like a slave because the money ain't enough to get us by. You shouldn't have to struggle like this, Ma!" He paused to catch his breath.

He saw Gloria was about to say something, but he stopped her before she spoke. "Don't interrupt me, Ma. Let me finish."

Gloria was speechless, because her son had turned into a man right before her eyes, and he was exerting his authority. Any other time she would have checked his ass, but for some reason, all she could do was respect it. Gloria remained quiet and allowed him to continue.

"I've been hustling, Ma. I know you don't approve, but I'm not about to stop until I know we straight. Don't ask about school because that's a done deal. Nobody is going to help us financially and you said yourself, we're not going on welfare. All I need for you to do is trust me and everything will be alright." He stepped back away from her arms reach and waited for the repercussions of what he had just said.

As this reality show played out in the living room, Brandon was standing in the corner dumbfounded. He just heard his brother tell their mother that he was selling drugs. He knew that was wrong and he couldn't understand why his brother would do such a thing.

Not fully understanding the adult conversation that had just occurred in front of him, Brandon wanted to express his displeasure in knowing that his big brother was doing something wrong. Stepping from the confines of his corner, he emerged as if he was a superhero there to save the day.

"Ma, are you just going…"

Before the rest of his statement could be completed Gloria cut her eyes in his direction and glared at him.

"Boy, you shut your mouth right now! I know what you're about to say, but you best not say anything! You hear me! As a matter of fact…" she paused, then turned to face Brandon eye to eye, so that he understood that she meant what she was about to say. "Don't you mention this conversation to nobody outside the walls of this house! What goes on in here is nobody's business! Do you understand me young man?" Gloria demanded.

Brandon was dumbfounded, but he answered his mother. "Yes, Mam." He nodded his head for added obedience showing he understood what she said. He knew better than to disobey his mother's wishes. He had a lot of questions and he realized that there were not about to be answered at that point.

Gloria hugged her baby boy. "Ok baby. Why don't you go in your bedroom and finish up your homework while I cook us dinner. When we sit down to eat, I want to hear all about your day at school. But right now I need to have a private conversation with Malik."

Brandon and his mother finished hugging, however, he was now upset. He was mad because his mother was putting him on the back burner to deal with Malik's crap and what he'd done. The entire situation that had taken place had gotten him pissed off and feeling neglected. *Why am I the one getting sent to my room? He's the on selling drugs and dropping out of school.* He was so disgusted that he didn't even open his mouth to say anything further. He just turned away filled with resentment.

As Brandon made the short walk to his bedroom, he looked over his shoulder at his brother. It was like he was moving in slow motion and his expression showed an emotion he'd never had before. Because neither Malik nor Gloria was looking directly at him. They couldn't see the look of envy and jealously that burned in his eyes at his mother choosing Malik over him.

That confession from Malik started the delusional and unwarranted confrontation in his mind between him and his brother. It was in that moment, that Brandon made it up in his child's mind, that his mother favored and loved Malik more. Because his thoughts were his own, no one was able to see the hatred that he'd just developed for a brother that wanted nothing more than to provide for him and protect him.

CHAPTER 3

Malik stood on the stoop waiting for his ride. He was in a good mood knowing he had been able to help pull his family out of financial debt. Although his mother made it clear that she didn't approve of what he did, she understood why he had done it and always made it her business to let him know that she loved and appreciated him. But he would only smile and say it was for the family.

The truth of the matter was that he'd already become the 'go to' dude for pills and that 'good good' in his neighborhood. Although, he'd been a good student in school, he was better at getting money. He'd only had a year left in school, but because his business was becoming a lucrative avenue for him, Malik knew he needed to devote his full attention to making it work. He'd done something that he knew was against everything that his parents stood for, but Malik had entered into the realm of manhood with the weight of the world on his shoulders. With manhood came difficult choices and decisions, and with that mindset he had dropped out of high school.

For three years he flipped his money, studied, took notes and watched how the game was being played. His eyes were wider than that block that he was running. His eyes were on a bigger prize — the takeover of the whole damn city.

The ride Malik had been waiting for finally came and he climbed into the black Camero and greeted his right hand man Rich. They had gone to school together and found themselves in similar situations with the streets as their only way out.

"Damn, man. What took you so long to get here?" he asked, turning down the music.

Nasir Richards, known on the streets as Rich, was slumped down in his seat with his hat pulled low. He was dark skin with sleepy, sexy eyes, and full lips. He was always serious and rarely smiled. He and Malik had become friends when they were in grade school playing baseball.

"I had to drop off this shorty I had with me. You can't bring no bitch to the mall son. They think you supposed to buy them something and shit. Or they might start asking for shit," he said in a flat tone.

Malik shook his head and laughed. "You ain't shit son."

Rich rolled down his window down and pressed the button to turn his music back up. "Never claimed to be my nigga," he said just as the sound of Drake blasted through the car speakers.

~~~~

After spending an enormous amount of cash at the mall, Malik was finally on his way back home. He couldn't wait to get home and show his mother what he'd gotten her and Brandon. It had been a long time since they had received really good gifts. He couldn't wait to see their faces.

He especially couldn't wait to see Brandon, who was finally coming home for a visit from school. A while ago, he had been accepted into a private school that would allow him to stay on campus and with his help, was able to attend. Malik felt good that at least one of them would finish high school and go to college. Although Brandon had been a little reluctant to leave their mother, Malik had made it clear it wasn't an option. He assumed Brandon was scared to be on his own and would become homesick. However, Brandon's reasons were totally different. He believed Malik wanted to send him away to school to get rid of him.

With the sense of abandonment and isolation rushing through him Brandon became aloof and indifferent to his brother. His mother's constant appraisal of Malik didn't help matters either. The more he called home the more he had to listen to her brag about something Malik bought her or fixed up in the house. It had become so bad that his phone calls dropped from four times a week to only once a week. The excuse he gave her was that his classes required more of his attention, but the truth is that he was sick of hearing about Malik. A younger brother should idolized and worship their older brother, but in Brandons' mind Malik had become his competition. His nemesis.

~~~~

When Brandon got home, he was pulled into a bear hug by his mother and brother. He loves the attention from his mother, but was a little distant to Malik. Malik and Gloria didn't even notice because they were so excited to see him. Gloria had him tell her about everything and he was on cloud nine thinking he'd finally be the center of attention again.

"Baby, did you decide where you want to go to college? I hope you made some good choices," said Gloria as she placed another piece of fried chicken on his plate.

They were sitting in the dining room of their new apartment courtesy of Malik. When he packed them up to move, he told her it was so that she would feel safer coming home from work.

Brandon felt a pang of anger at his mother's question. He remembered the day at school when his class chose and filled out their college applications. He'd never been so disappointed and furious.

"Yeah, I did. I had to do it on my own since the staff decided they were only handing out community college applications or technical applications to the black students."

"What! Those racist bastards!" yelled Gloria, defending her son.

"Are you sure about that. Maybe she missed placing some of the applications on your desk," said Malik. He didn't want to believe that Brandon was being mistreated at the school.

Brandon smiled at his mother loving the maternal feeling of her protecting him. He then looked at Malik, his smile gone. "I'm sure," he said in a flat tone. "There's only one other black student in my class and he received the same treatment. All the other students received applications from all the top school. It didn't even matter to them that we are in the top ten ranking of the whole school."

"You know what. I'm going to call the school and speak to someone. This is an outrage. How the hell can they treat kids that way?" asked Gloria upset.

"Easy. I'm a young black man, that's bound for an ivy league school, and in the future may hold an illustrious position in a prestigious company. They're threatened by that."

"Well, I'm still going to call," she said with a frown.

Malik laughed. "Ma, don't call the school. I'm sure Brandon can stand up on his own two feet and handle this himself. All he has to do is write to the school and request an application and fill it out on his own. End of problem."

Gloria smiled and reached out to pat Malik's hand. "I guess you're right," she said and took Brands hand with her other.

Malik picked up his glass. "I mean it's not that hard. It's not like he cried about it or anything," said Malik before taking a few swallows of his fruity drink.

Brandon's body tensed. Hot humiliating anger rushed through him and his eyes narrowed. He knew there was no way that Malik knew that he had in fact went back to his room and sat in the bathroom and cried. It was tears of frustration, anger and helplessness. It didn't mean that he was a baby or a coward. But when he thought about how Malik would have handled it, he felt like an imbecile and he hated Malik even more for making him realize it.

"Oh, I almost forgot." Malik reached into his pocket and pulled out a small envelope. "I got you something."

"Boy, you've done enough Malik. Stop buying me stuff," she said, pushing the envelope back towards him on the table.

Malik hunched his shoulder's. "Alright then. I guess you don't want to go see Mary Mary in concert down at NJPAC."

"Wait, who? Boy, give me those tickets!" she said, snatching them back.

Malik laughed. "There's two in there. I thought you might want to take Mrs. Gibbs with you."

Gloria opened the envelope beaming at the two fourth row tickets. "Yesssss… She is gonna love this. Thank you baby!" she said, leaning over and kissing his cheek loudly.

"I got this for you little brother," Malik said, sliding a black card over towards Brandon.

Brandon gazed down at the credit card, not touching it. "Why?"

Malik smiled, "Because I can that's why. Besides, you deserve it. Ma shows me all of your report cards. I'm proud of you. So now you'll have enough money to take out one of those little girls you're always telling Ma about."

Brandon never told his mother he had dumped his last girlfriend after finding out she only went out with him to see how black guys fuck. When he found out he made sure he fucked her brains out for the whole night before dumping her.

"Well, aren't you going to say thank you?" asked Gloria. *He's been acting strange lately and I can't put my finger on as to why.*

"Yes, thank you, Malik," he said with a nod.

Malik nodded back. *He's growing up. Usually he'd be all excited about receiving gifts. Now he's all laid back,* thought Malik.

"Ma, I gotta go," said Malik standing.

"Already? Brandon just got here," she said, putting down her glass.

"I know," he said grinning. "I'll be back tomorrow. He's not going anywhere, are you?" he asked, smiling over at Brandon.

Brandon stared at him and then gave him a fake smile. *I bet you would like that, wouldn't you.* "Nope. Never."

Malik laughed. "See, Ma. I told you." He leaned down and placed a kiss on her cheek.

"Well, what time will you be here tomorrow?" she asked curiously. "If you come in the morning I'll make breakfast."

"I can cook my own breakfast, you know," said Malik teasingly.

I'm here. How come she isn't all excited about making me breakfast? "You don't live here anymore?" Brandon asked confused.

Malik and Gloria both looked at him like he had lost his mind.

"Brandon, I wrote to you last month and told you I got my own little spot. Didn't you get my letter? I mean, Ma said that you're too busy to write back because of all your classes, so I don't always know."

Brandon looked over at his mother. He knew he didn't tell her that for Malik's sake, but he didn't say so now. "Oh yeah. I guess it slipped my mind."

Malik laughed. "I guess they really are working your butt off then, huh?"

Malik walked over to the wall unit and pulled down a silver box. After lifting the lid, he pulled a large roll of money from his pocket and dropped it inside.

Brandon ignored Malik's comment. He watched as he put the money in the box and returned it to the shelf. "You still a drug dealer?" he said without trying to hide his disgust.

"Brandon!" Gloria snapped.

Malik's smile dropped for a brief second, but he managed to keep it in place. "Aren't you still in that fancy school I pay for? Don't you still have college to get through?" When Brandon responded with silence, Malik nodded. "Well, there you go. See you tomorrow Ma. Little brother."

Malik left, closing the door behind him. He walked down the stairs trying to figure out if his brother had just tried to play him.

FALSE

Suddenly, he smiled and shook it off. *I'm reading too much into it. That's my little man.*

CHAPTER 4

Brandon woke up that morning with a splitting headache blurring his vision for a second. What the fuck even happened last night? Short scenes flashed before his eyes, as he rubbed them in his attempt to soothe the pain. He saw himself and a couple of girls grinding on the dance floor. He then saw one of them pulling him upstairs and undressing him. The rest was a blur, but he got a pleasant feeling from it so it must've been good.

He remembered a couple of guys from the neighborhood he used to hang with inviting him to a party. Ecstatic that they even wanted him around, he quickly accepted. Although he only could remember bits and pieces of his time there, he was glad that he went.

Brandon drew in a deep breath trying to let the after effects of his wild night ease from his body. Feeling the burning irritation of a scratchy, dry throat, he reached for the glass of water on the nightstand and gulped the liquid down within a matter of seconds. After his pain soothed a bit, he got dressed and headed towards the kitchen.

He could hear voices from below and knew Malik was there. His brother's peals of laughter could be heard clearly even through closed doors. He felt disgusted. Why did he always have to be so happy? He was fuckin' scum. A drug dealer. He should be lying in a corner and hating himself for what he did to people, not spending his time in the kitchen, laughing with their mother as if he was some kind of saint.

"Morning, sunshine," his mother joked when he strolled into the kitchen. "Wild party last night, huh?"

He stared at her in confusion.

"He don't know shit, Ma," Malik laughed. "I went there as soon as they got snitched on."

"What are you talking about?" asked Brandon frowning.

He was genuinely confused. He forgot about the hatred towards his brother only for a second as he tried to understand. Maybe he'd find out what actually happened that made his head hurt like shit.

"Some of your homies got their party favors from me," Malik explained, sipping on his coffee. "Someone snitched and the cops busted the party, but I got you out of there before you got caught. The funny thing is, you didn't take no drugs," he chuckled. "You were just drunk as fuck."

Malik's last words were filled with an odd kind of pride. Sure, he didn't agree with his little brother drinking his brains out, but despite being surrounded by drugs at the party, he hadn't touched any. None.

Brandon didn't hear pride, though. All he could hear was his older brother *'the fucking drug dealer'* making fun of him. He had the nerve to be applauding him for not succumbing to that disgusting plague that he helped spread. When Malik reached up and patted the top of his head, he moved back, an annoyed look on his face. He headed to the fridge and pulled out some cold pancakes. He started to munch on them as he made his way to the table and sat down.

"Hey, I ain't judging," Malik told him, not aware of the true reason of Brandon's indignation. "Last day of school. Last party night with your boys. It's all good. I get it."

"It's not all good from my point of view," Gloria suddenly spoke, prompting startled jumps from her sons. They had forgotten they weren't alone. "You still drank so much you forgot your own name. And if it wasn't for your brother who got you out of there, we'd have to get your ass out of jail. You should thank him instead of giving him attitude."

Brandon felt the rage building inside him stronger and hotter than before. He felt the embarrassment mixed with anger burning him down to the bone. Malik. It was always Malik. No matter what he or someone else did, his mother would always have to sneak a little *'Malik-praising'* into the conversation.

Why couldn't she do that for him? Couldn't she see that everything his older brother was doing was completely wrong? Why did she keep praising him as if he was some fucking Hollywood star? All he did was drink and have a little fun, like any guy his age would've. And yet, he was still the one getting scolded.

That's it, he thought. He needed to get out. He needed to clear his mind and somehow calm himself down.

"I'm going out," he announced abruptly as he left the kitchen. Moments later, Malik and Gloria heard the front door slam as he left.

Fuck. He slammed his fist against the hard concrete wall he passed. *Fuck, fuck, fuck!* He walked down the street without a destination in mind. He just needed to get away from the house.

A blast of heated thoughts moved through his head as he continued to move aimlessly down the street. Brandon looked up twenty minutes later not knowing how he got to Hopkins Street. He looked around him at the wilted neighborhood and only saw depression and hopelessness.

Kids were running around playing in a lot next to an abandoned building. On the corner a few guys were standing around waiting for their next sale. A bunch of men was lined up against the wall of the liquor store sipping on their bottles and swapping the same old stories.

This was the hood. The ghetto. And it all belonged to Malik. He ran it all. *Damn, why didn't I think to sell drugs too. I'm way smarter than Malik. If I would've thought of it first, this would all belong to me. I would've been the king of the streets now and I would be the one receiving all their mothers love and attention.*

Brandon felt the sting of tears and hastily blinked them away. *This could still be mine. It would just take some planning.* Suddenly, a strange, sick little smile played across his face. It was time to steal the so called king's crown.

~~~~

"So what are ya gonna do now?" Jaymes asked, dragging one last pull from his cigarette before throwing it in the small puddle in front of him much to Brandon's joy. He had never smelled anything worse than cigarette smoke.

"I'm gonna…" he paused. He didn't like what he was going to say at all. "I'm gonna be like him." The last three words hurt him more than any knife or gun would have. *Be like him.* It still echoed in his head, driving him mad with anger.

"You're crazy," the other boy said, seemingly careless. "You've heard the stories and ya know better than anyone what he can do. Haven't ya heard what he did to old man Carter?"

Brandon's ears perked up. That was new.

"What?"

"He refused to pay for his tab," Jaymes smirked. "For a long time too. Apparently, he was going to leave the city yesterday, but your bro got to him first."

"What did he do to him?" Brandon asked, hating himself for the sincere curiosity he displayed.

"Let's just say old man Carter has nothing to run with now." With yet another smirk, Jaymes pointed to his legs, his lips mimicking the sound of a gunshot. *Pop! Pop!*

Brandon stifled a shudder. He knew what his brother could do and he even heard Malik himself talking about it a few times with their mother, but he couldn't quite accept it yet. In fact, he wasn't sure he was ever going to.

"Still wanna join the gang?" asked Jaymes.

"Yeah. I'm not scared. I want to see for myself."

"Then I guess we gotta find us some connections."

"Oh, don't worry," Brandon assured his friend. "With my brother's rep, I'm pretty sure we're not going to have any problems with that."

~~~~

Two days later...

Luckily for Brandon, the evening's gloom did a great job at hiding his nervousness. He was leading his friends into a gang he heard his brother talking about the other night. Apparently, that was the place one of the hustlas did his business.

Jaymes was confident as usual, unlike the other guy, Dominik, who chose to only stare at the concrete while he walked. It kind of annoyed Brandon, to be honest. He felt like Dominiks' fear would drag him down and ultimately, it would end up getting them all in trouble. He was starting to regret bringing him. Jaymes alone would've been perfect.

They found Vice in a small bar that was used by the dealers as a meeting spot. He knew he was probably making a very big mistake walking in there as if he owned the place, but that was the only way he could earn some respect from his first try. And if that didn't work, he could always say that he was there on his brother's behalf, as much as he despised the idea.

The man in question stood at a table in a darker corner of the bar, a dirty glass filled with a dark brown liquid in front of him. He gulped it down when he saw the young boys. He glared at them in a mix of curiosity and irritation as they sat down in front of him.

"I ain't got nothing for your bro," Vice spat. "I paid him last week, so y'all can get the fuck outta my face."

Brandon had no idea what he was talking about. But luckily, he knew how to play his part.

"I know that," he spoke calmly, fixing Vice with an icy look. "We came for work."

"What?"

"Ya heard me right," Brandon said, trying to adopt Jaymes way of talking. His ivy league school education was pushed to the back burner as he tried to sound hood. "We wanna work for you, and it ain't got nothing to do with my brother either."

Vice's face cracked into a grin, his yellow teeth making Brandon want to gag. He stared at the three young boys sitting before him and knew he could use them as runners. The police wouldn't look at them twice because of their innocent faces.

"A'ight," he finally said after he'd carefully thought over his plan. "I got a special delivery tonight for one of the big boys down on Wilbur Avenue. Y'all sure about this?"

"Mad sure," Brandon replied, his words emphasized by his boys nodding their heads. "We'll do it."

"A'ight then. But if you fuck this up, I'll put two in each of you. Ya feel me?" The boys nodded and Vice continued, pulling a small white package from an inner pocket of his coat and sliding it to Brandon. "Ya know where the mayor lives?"

Brandon drew his hand back from the package scowling. "You want me to take that to the mayor? He's gonna get us fucking locked up!"

Vice laughed at the fear on his face. "Nah...Ol' Jameson's one of us," he said leaning back. "He's havin' a pretty big party tonight and he wants his shit right away. My main running ain't get back yet, so you can make this one." He shoved the package closer to him. "Now go and don't come back until you have my money."

With nothing else left to be said, Brandon took the package and shoved it in the book bag he was carrying. When he stood up, the other boys followed and they quickly left the bar. No one paid them any attention as they walked out carrying five thousand dollars worth of Molly's. Either they didn't notice or they didn't care.

"Ya think it would be better if only one of us delivered this shit?" Dominik asked, casting nervous glances at the book bag. Brandon had been expecting this question from him and surprisingly, he was glad he asked.

"You fuckin' pussy," Jaymes said and laughed. "You begged me to come and now you punking out."

"I was just sayin', man," he shrugged. "It's gonna look suspicious as fuck if all three of us walk to the house like, *Hey man, want some of this?*"

Jaymes opened his mouth for another joke, but was quickly interrupted by Brandon.

"Nah, he's right. We're gonna look like dumbasses and then, if we don't get locked up by the mayor, we gon' get our asses shanked by Vice and his crew."

"Then who's gonna deliver?"

"Me," came Brandon's short response. "I have my brother's respect behind me as a shield, so if something goes wrong, nothing will happen to me. I can't say the same about y'all, though."

Brandon was pleased to see his friends' concerned faces. They seemed to agree with him and ultimately, gave in. He had wanted to convince them to give up and was happy when they did. That night belonged to him, and him alone. There was no place for mistakes.

Thoughts of the money he was about to make had him feeling anxious. He could already see himself covering his mother in gifts and receiving all her love and attention. He saw himself being hugged and praised by her, while Malik sat in a corner looking foolish. He could see him glaring at them with jealousy, like Brandon had done so many times before.

"A'ight then," Jaymes finally spoke up. "You on your own, Bruh. Just let me know if you need me though."

"I got this," said Brandon, trying to hide his enthusiasm after seeing his plan work.

"But we're gonna get a share of that cash, feel me?" said Jaymes not really asking. He gave Brandon a hard stare, waiting for his reply.

"Don't worry man. I got'chu," Brandon assured them. They could have it all as far as he was concerned. He was gonna make more than that if his plan worked.

Jaymes nodded and he and Dominik started walking in the opposite direction.

As soon as he was left alone, Brandon headed straight to the mayor's house. It was definitely bigger than the average neighborhood house and it was surrounded by a tall concrete fence. There was no way he could sneak in so he decided to take the obvious way – the main gate. There was a small speaker installed on the wall with a red button that read *'Push to speak'*. He pushed the button and waited for someone to answer.

"Business or simple visit?" a woman's voice echoed through the box as soon as he pressed the button.

"Business."

The gates instantly opened, leaving him enough space to get inside the yard. He walked along the pavement and glanced at the tall trees that framed it. *Ol' Jameson surely had a taste for the fine life.* When he finally reached the door, he rang the bell and was soon greeted by a middle-aged man, obviously drunk.

"Who the fuck are you?" he said, struggling to tie together the question through gritted teeth.

"I've got a package for Jameson," Brandon replied, patting his pocket.

The expression on the man's face shifted in a matter of seconds.

"Come in," he said, moving aside so Brandon could get in.

The heavy smell of cigarettes and sweat struck him instantly. The living room was crowded with a colorful mass of people laughing and dancing as if they had no care in the world. He even saw a few men playing with the skirts of the girls who were grinding against them in their laps. They wore no underwear. Brandon eyes were glued to their asses.

"So, boy," he heard the drunken man's voice snapping his attention back to business. "What d'you have for me?"

"The package from Vice."

"Follow me."

He seemed less drunk as he walked upstairs closely followed by Brandon. When they finally stopped, he turned to him and demanded to see the pack. Brandon handed it to him and could barely hold back a chuckle when the man sniffed it as if he could actually test its authenticity like that.

He seemed pleased, though.

"Good, good," he murmured. He reached into the pocket of his bathrobe and pulled out a thick stack of cash. "Five thousand," he said, slapping the banknotes hard against Brandon's hand. "Now get out. And tell Vice I'll need a fresh batch next month around this time."

As he walked out, Brandon could barely contain his excitement. Five thousand dollars. He had just easily earned five thousand dollars. Sure, he had to give the biggest part to Vice and then share what was left between himself and his friends, but it had still been easy money.

When Brandon finally returned to the bar, he handed Vice the money. He sat there quietly as he watched him count it. Nodding his head, he peeled off a few bills and tossed them on the table in front of him. Vice decided that he should only have seven hundred dollars for the run. Brandon found that a bit unfair, but didn't argue back. He figured that he would give his two friends only one hundred each since they didn't do shit and keep the rest for himself.

He snatched the money up and stuffed it into his pocket. As he left the bar, he had a huge grin on his face. *Like I said. Easy money.*

~~~~

It seemed that Brandon's fame was growing day by day. He delivered packages for the small time dealers and met the important people in the city. It came as no surprise to him to see how many of the high-ranking men and women depended on his services. At the end of every delivery he would get a hefty sum and he was happy with it, mostly because he could now buy his mother things as well. Gloria had been grateful at first, thinking the gifts were bought from his savings, but when they started arriving more often and getting more expensive, she started getting suspicious and reached out to Malik.

"I don't know where he gets the money from," she told Malik one day, pointing to the box full of jewelry Brandon had given her.

Malik didn't know either, but he was going to find out what was going on.

"Don't worry, Ma," he told her. "I'll find out and handle it."

Gloria smiled already feeling relief. Malik's pulled her into his arms and gave her a hug.

"I have to go, Ma. I'll call you later, okay?"

"Alright, baby. Be safe in those streets," she said, holding on for a moment longer.

"Always," said Malik. He squeezed her tightly and kissed her cheek one last time with a loud smacking sound before leaving the house.

His plan was to wait for Brandon to leave and follow him. He hid on the side of a small brick house down the street and waited patiently. He was well hidden due to his dark clothes which he used to his advantage. Fortunately, he didn't have to wait long.

After a few minutes, he saw Brandon come into view on the porch. He watched as he locked the front door, descended the few steps, and headed down the block in a hurry. Malik followed him closely from the opposite side of the street. Luckily for him, Brandon didn't pay attention to what was going on around him. *What a mistake*, Malik thought, shaking his head.

As expected, Brandon took the road that led to the center of the city, the same place he started his own 'career' in. His blood was boiling. His little brother, whom he thought incapable of doing such things, was heading straight to Vice's pub and went in as if he owned the place.

I'll show him who really owns everything around here, he thought as he got his phone out. After a few calls, and about ten minutes, he was surrounded by some of his most trusted men. Trey, Meek and Rock, each bigger and tougher looking than the other. They were always strapped and ready for whatever. They had murder in their eyes and fire flowing through their veins. None of them had ever liked Vice and this opportunity was too good to pass.

"I'll go in first," Malik instructed them. "I just wanna make sure before we off them motherfuckers. Y'all come in at my signal."

The men nodded and with a blank expression plastered on his face, he entered the pub.

"Sup, Vicey boy," he laughed as he sat down at the table next to his brother who instantly tensed up in fear. "I see you're here with my lil' bro and by the looks of it, y'all ain't playin' Monopoly."

His gaze swerved across the colorful packs spread on the table. There were at least fifteen types of drugs there, all sorted by a different color. He knew better than anyone how Vice worked, since he copped most of his shit from him.

"He came to me," Vice shrugged, trying to seem unaffected about the tension that was evident all around them.

"Oh, he did, huh?"

Even with the smile on Malik's face, Vice wasn't stupid. The ice in Malik's eyes told a different story.

Turning to his brother Malik continued to grin. "You did?"

The only reaction that came from Brandon was a small nod.

Weirdly enough, Malik was happy to see the fear in his brother's eyes. Maybe that would convince him why this wasn't the right choice for him. To stay the fuck in school and leave the streets to him.

"I see how it is," Malik hissed, the first sign of his anger being shown. With a hand wave the pub's doors were slammed open by his men, who wasted no time in shooting everything and everyone that moved, except the bartender. She cowered in fear behind the counter waiting for her turn. It never came, though.

The three men stepped over the still-twitching bodies on the floor and when they finally reached Malik's table, they stood still in silence.

"Now what do I do with my boy Vice here?" Malik smirked, his eyes glaring devilishly at the terrified man in front of him. "You know what? I'll deal with you myself, but before I do," he uttered, turning to face the woman behind the bar. "I want you to tell everyone that will listen that if they try and give my brother work, then I'll have to come and put in *work*. You got that?"

The woman nodded and ran out of the bar, stumbling over the lifeless bodies as she headed for the door. Malik felt bad for her. By the looks of it, she wasn't used to seeing this kind of shit. Which was quite odd, considering her work place.

That being said, he pulled out his knife and with a quick hand movement, he slit Vice's throat. Blood sprayed his hands and Brandon's face as he let out a disgusting gurgling sound before falling head first on the table.

"If I catch you again," he said, turning to Brandon, who was staring wide-eyed at him. "I'm gonna beat the shit outta you in front of Ma. Understood?"

Brandon gave a weak nod. It was all he could do at that moment and he hated it. He hated how weak he was in front of his brother.

"Good. I'm not gonna tell her anything this time. But I'm dead serious about what I said."

He grabbed a bunch of napkins from the tabled, wiped off his knife and then cleaned his hands. "Meek, call Stacey and tell him we have a clean up at Vice's place. Tell him to send a replacement too."

"You got it Malik," said Meek, walking away to make the call.

Malik stood up and Brandon followed like a scared little boy.

"Trey, take him to the Den and let him get cleaned up. Then take him home." He glanced back over his shoulder at Brandon. "Don't give Trey any trouble. Do as he says and don't upset Mom when you get in the house. You got that?"

Brandon nodded, bested by his brother once again. The sharp knife of anger wedging even deeper.

CHAPTER 5

Three weeks had passed since Vice's death and as expected, no one said a thing. From what Brandon saw that day, Malik took over Vice's territory, and his clients as well. The money was flowing in double time now, especially with all Vice's high society customers.

This made Brandon even angrier than he already was. He was 17, damnit! Almost 18 and technically, he was an adult. He was tired of seeing his brother basking in street fame and cash while he had to waste time in a classroom surrounded by loud racist idiots.

Of course, the events hadn't just passed by unnoticed. Everyone knew about Brandon and his overprotective older brother. Some people made fun of him, laughing at him as if he had been some kind of kid who needed chastising.

The most annoying moments in Brandon's opinion are the ones when he's walking to class and other students that use to talk to him pass by him in fear. They are so afraid that they would cower in fear as they hurry along. The thing that drove him mad was that the respect wasn't even fairly earned by him, but by Malik. They were afraid of his brother, and by extension, scared of him.

It was all because of Malik. Wherever he went, that's all he heard. Malik did this, Malik said that. Malik, Malik, Malik. Even his mother, the person he loved the most in the world, seemed to ignore him lately. *I'm sick of being in his shadow,"* as he stood near the school's front gate.

Today, Malik had called and said he would be picking him up from school instead of him taking the usual bus ride home. It annoyed him, of course, but there was no way he could refuse. Truth was, despite all the hatred he felt for Malik, he was still afraid of him. Especially after he saw what he could really do.

He hadn't been waiting long before a newly bought black Dodge Viper stopped in front of the school yard prompting amazed gasps from the kids that saw it. He rolled his eyes and quickly got into the car, making himself comfortable on the black leather covered back seat. The front seat was occupied by a blonde bimbo who looked like she had just been taken out of a strip club. Knowing his brother, that was probably true. She didn't even look at him, let alone say hello.

"Sup, Brandon?" Malik said with a smile.

"Nothing."

"Oh, C'mon. There can't really be nothing going on. How was your d…"

"It was fine," Brandon snapped. "Now pay attention to the fuckin' road or you're gonna get us killed."

Malik was shocked. It was the first time he heard his brother talk like that and he wasn't sure he liked it. Especially in front of that chick. She was gonna think he was some weak piece of shit now all because Brandon decided to try him.

"You'd better not talk like that around Ma," he threatened.

"Why do you give a shit? You don't live there to hear it."

Malik took a deep breath, his fingers tightening their grip around the wheel. For some reason Brandon was angry and he couldn't figure out why. He thought showing up in a flashy car in front of his friends would make him feel like a boss. Wasn't every high school boy's dream to be seen in a car like that? Hell, he even risked exposing one of his hoes to him. It seemed that it all had been in vain.

"Look, I ain't got time for this," he spoke as calmly as he could. "But we gon' talk tonight, okay?"

"You're not Dad," Brandon mumbled from the back seat.

Malik's eyes shot up to the review mirror to see Brandon behind him. "What the fuck you say?"

"I said you're not Dad!" Brandon shouted, sheer rage filling his voice. "You're not Dad and you'll never be. You know what he'd do if he knew what you're doing right now? He'd fuckin' spit on you, that's what he'd…"

In a quick movement Malik swerved the car over to the curb and stopped. He unlocked the doors and looked back over his shoulder at Brandon. "Get out," he spat through gritted teeth. "Get out before I do something I might regret."

Brandon laughed. He felt unusually powerful as he did that. Seeing his brother get angry because of him and watching him struggle to contain the fire that was eating at him, made Brandon feel like a God.

"So now you're gonna kill me too?" he snorted. "Like you did Vice?"

That was it. Blinded by fury, Malik got out of the car and walked around to the back seat. He didn't even open the back door. He dragged Brandon out of the car through the window, then reclaimed his seat at the wheel, and drove away.

He left Brandon lying on the concrete, his clothes a mess, but feeling happier than he had ever felt. If that's what being the boss felt like, he now understood why Malik fought so hard to keep his position. Brandon smiled evilly as the adrenaline rushed through him. *How'd you like that shit, bro?*

~~~~

It was late in the evening when Brandon heard someone turning his door knob. He was sitting at his desk when Malik opened the door and stepped in. He pretended not to see him, hoping he'd go away as he flipped through the latest issue of *Deadpool.*

"*The Merc With A Mouth,* huh?" Malik smiled as he read the title. Lately it seemed like Brandon was rushing the idea of growing up, but then there were times like this when he would catch him reading comic books that made him hope otherwise. He wished he could just understand that he wanted him to be safe and for his life to turn out better than his.

Brandon grimaced. *Why did he feel the need to ruin such a perfect day?*

"Look," he continued, looking uncomfortable sitting on Brandon's bed. "I just wanted to apologize about everything."

Silence.

"You know I do what I do because I care about you and Ma," he sighed. "I just want a better life for you two. You're my lil bro and I wanna take care of you as best as I can."

Again, no answer. There was nothing but the soft sound of pages being turned.

"I don't want you to take the same path I did," said Malik. "It's not for you."

"Who are you to decide that?" Brandon finally spoke, feeling the hatred growing inside of him. "Who are you to tell me what I can and can't do, huh?"

"Your older brother."

Brandon snorted.

"Again, you're not Dad and you'll never be like him. So just give up."

A loud sigh escaped Malik's throat.

"No, I'm not like him," he said, looking down in shame. "I don't even dare to say that I am. And I know I'll never be like him. He was so… honest and fair and I'm just…"

"A dirty hustla," he said in disgust.

Malik nodded. "Yeah, that's it. A dirty hustla doing his best to keep his little brother in school and pay for the roof over his head," Malik added, the faint pride note in his tone making Brandon sick.

"Get outta my room," he said, calmly turning the page to read the next chapter. *Carnage was totally going to get mauled in this one*, he thought with a smile, now focused back on his reading. Carnage was his least favorite character. He only thought about his own personal pleasure and acted in such a way that he ignored everyone around him.

"I'm not gonna leave until we're through with this," said Malik. He seemed much angrier than before and Brandon seemed pleased with it. He had never been a patient man and Brandon knew exactly how to play with that.

"Well, your ass is going to rot here, cause I don't feel like talking to you today."

"Brandon, if only…"

"If only what?" he snapped, cutting him off. "If only what, huh? If only I listened to you complaining about how hard your life is and how we should feel bad for your sorry ass? If only I would cry for you when you drive all those fancy ass cars and spending all your cash?"

"Brandon…"

But he was only just getting started. All the last few weeks frustrations was coming out and there was nothing he could do to stop it.

"If only I pitied you when I saw you stacking the money as if it was simple to get that much paper? Or when I caught you fucking that big-tittied whore in the back seat of your new Audi? Fuck off, Malik," he spat. "I don't want any of your shit. I'm a grown ass ma…"

A loud whack ended his discourse, followed by a stinging pain in his cheek. The realization that he was no longer on his chair, but on the floor, shocked him. He stared up at his brother and seeing the pure anger in his eyes, he felt afraid once again. He despised himself for that.

"You fuckin' bastard," he groaned. "You hit me. You hit me!" he yelled.

"I had to," Malik said, panting. "You wouldn't listen. I'm sorry, Brandon. I really am."

He helped him up and after he sat him back down in his chair, Malik continued.

"Just do as I say and keep studying. You'll become a big man someday and you need to be educated for that. You can't have that if you fuck with these streets."

He moved towards the door and stopped when a thought came to mind. He knew Brandon was stubborn as fuck, so he felt he should scare him a bit to keep him from trying to be a hustla again.

"And I swear, if I catch you doing any illegal shit again, I'll kill you myself."

He knew he didn't mean a word of it, but it needed to be said. With a chuckle, he left the room, leaving behind a more confused than ever Brandon.

Did he seriously think he could just do that? Did he actually believe he could just say shit like that and get away with it like nothing happened?

I'll show him. I'll show him and everyone else who's the biggest, meanest motherfucker around. Just wait and see, Malik, he thought. *Just wait and see.*

CHAPTER 6

This was the big day for Brandon. It was graduation day. The day he would finally get to see his classmates for the last time. How he hated them. He hated them all for the admiration they had for his brother. He hated them all for wanting to be his friend because of him. He hated the fact that they believed his low life hustla brother was someone to idolize.

That night after his brother hit him it all became clear to him. He decided that since he couldn't join his brother on the streets, he would dedicate the rest of his life trying to take the streets from him. It would please him like nothing else to ruin Malik's life.

He would destroy him and his empire little by little. He would start with the small corner thugs, ending with the ones that sat in his trap houses throughout the day bagging drugs and counting all his money. That's what mattered most to Malik—his money. And he would do whatever it takes to rip it from his grasp.

Suddenly his thoughts turned to their mother and he smiled. His desire to impress her has never faded. It's only gotten stronger, almost becoming an obsession. And even though his need to have her love all to himself is what drives him, his only wish at the current moment was to do everything he could to destroy his brother's. To knock that ever present smug smile from his lips.

He wanted to see him crawling in the dirt begging him for his help. He wanted to strip him of his power and respect and show everyone who he truly was – just a scared little man that used drug money to steal away all of their mother's affection. In Brandon's eyes, he was a coward. The exact opposite of everything their father raised them to be.

Brandon looked around the crowded lobby until he found his mother. He stood there watching as she scanned the crowd looking for him. As soon as their eyes met he stepped from the auditorium and began walking in her direction.

"My baby boy." Gloria kissed his forehead when he finally reached her. His graduation hat slid to the side when she hugged him tightly. "I'm so proud of you. So proud," she said, giving him one last squeeze.

"You did it, lil man," Malik said, patting his back. "So what are ya gonna do now?"

Brandon shrugged as if he didn't know, although he knew exactly what he was going to do. They were the ones that didn't know yet, mainly because they wouldn't approve. In fact, no one else knew about his plan. They had already begun pointing out different colleges for him to attend snatching the right to choose from his grasp. He heard his mother talking about Medical school the other night, to which his brother responded saying he should actually study law.

Brandon laughed inside. He had no idea how close he was to being right.

"Well, you have time to decide," Gloria said, taking his arm and guiding him outside to Malik's car; a new Lamborghini Aventador. The red race car was shining in the sunlight as the doors let out a slight hiss sound as they opened lifting towards the sky. *This beauty is going to be mine one day*, Brandon thought as he got into the luxury car.

For the first time in years, he actually felt happy that he was returning home. Gloria was throwing a graduation party for him that evening and it was the perfect cover up for what he was going to do.

"I've invited Amy too," she said, trying to sound innocent. Under other circumstances, Brandon would've gotten mad. Amy was his ex-girlfriend and she was obsessed with him. Despite his efforts to get his mother to believe it, she still thought the girl would make a great future wife. He shook his head. Amy wasn't good for nothing but a good time.

He just found it funny how his mother was already thinking about him getting married at such an early age and yet she never bothered Malik with the same stuff. *Probably because he wasn't worth the effort. Who the fuck wanted to marry a drug dealer with no future besides death or jail?*

"Whatever," Brandon said, gazing through the window watching as the night shadows started to creep in. Looking up at the sky, he noticed that it was also getting cloudy. *Perfect*, he thought.

When they finally arrived home, the lights were on and much to

Brandon's disappointment, the house was already full of partying teens and the music was booming through the speakers.

"Ma, this was really unnecessary," he sighed as he got out of the car. Hadn't he made it clear enough that he didn't want a big party? Sadly, and as usual, no one seemed to listen to anything he said, let alone actually take his opinion into consideration. He hated that about them. They never truly listened to him.

"Hey, hey," she said, giving him a tight hug. "It's your last day as a high schooler. You'd better make the best of it. Now go on in. Me and Malik are going to spend the night at your auntie's house."

Brandon couldn't believe his ears. They were actually leaving for the night. This couldn't have been better. Suddenly, his mood changed and he smiled.

"Alright then," he said and then kissed his mother's cheek. "I won't have too much fun."

"Don't have too much fun with Amy either," Malik said laughing.

With one last hug, Gloria stepped off the porch and headed back towards the car. Brandon didn't even bother to look at Malik or comment on what he'd said about Amy. He knew that this would be the last time he saw him before he started ruining his life. *I can't wait.*

~~~~

Everything seemed to be working perfectly so far. His mother and brother didn't show up to check on him as he thought they would and there were no thug faces at the party he recognized. He guessed his brother didn't want to ruin his fun by sending his people to spy on him.

But that didn't stop him from being cautious. Throughout the night when the attention would shift to someone else, he would sneak into his bedroom and pack a few things in his luggage. He did this quite a few times until he was happy with the contents of his bag.

During the last exit to his room, he made sure he had enough money for what he needed to do. He had been smart enough to save most of the money he made working for Vice, so he had a few thousand dollars to use. But when the time came, he would need to be smart how he spent it. In a few years he would need a place to stay, money to buy food and still have enough to pay his tuition. He made sure that his budget was perfectly split by his future needs and was happy with his results.

Once all of his luggage was packed, and the money hidden within a zippered section of the duffle bag, the last thing to do was find a way to sneak out without being noticed by the people in the house. The solution came disguised as Amy, his crazy ass ex. During the next hour, he began making advances to her friend Karen, who never left her side.

"You know," Amy said, looking at him in disapproval as he caressed Karen's thigh. "I didn't think you would get over our relationship that easily."

He didn't bother turning to her. He even pretended not to have heard her as his lips wandered along Karen's neck.

"You two never really had anything anyway," he heard Karen say. "Maybe that's why you let Malik fuck you in the back seat of his truck last year."

Although he wanted them to go at each other, Karen's response caught him off guard. His whole body tensed. He turned to look at Amy and from the irate stare she was throwing at Karen, he knew what she'd said to be the truth. Malik had fucked his girl. Okay, maybe at the time she had been his ex-girlfriend, but that shit still was wrong. It just proved to Brandon that he was correct about him. He was a piece of shit who really didn't give a fuck about him or anyone else.

Anger hot and sharp rushed through Brandon and he wanted nothing more than to wrap his hands around Amy's neck and squeeze the life out of her slutty ass. But he didn't want to fuck up his plan. *I'll just chuck it up as a casualty of war. I'll find my reward later when I set my plan into play.*

Much to his surprise Amy's response was pretty calm. "Your just jealous cause you've never fucked him," said Amy, quietly.

Keren giggle when Brandon tickled her ear with his tongue. "No, but I know who I'll be fucking later tonight," she said as she leaned over and kissed Brandon fully on the lips.

Amy got up fuming and Brandon smirked.

"I know you didn't just say that, you bitch," Amy snarled, pointing a perfectly manicured finger in Karen's face.

Karen got up as well and stepped up to Amy. Her face was so close Brandon could see her breath steaming up Amy's glasses.

"But I just did," she said all up in her face. "What you gonna do about it, huh?"

The answer came as a loud slap, followed by complete silence.

Everyone was paying attention to the girls now. They had even stopped the music so they could hear better.

It only took them half a second and a hatred-filled look at each other to start fighting. Much to Brandon's joy the people formed a tight circle around them, blocking their view of him. He was now safe from any inquisitive looks.

Carefully, he got up and walked to his bedroom. He looked back a few times to check if anyone had noticed his absence. They hadn't. They were too busy cheering for the two crazy bitches fighting over him.

He chuckled when he heard something break. It was the glass vase Malik brought their mother on her birthday a few years ago. Nothing brought him more happiness than knowing something his brother spent money on had broken.

Without turning the lights on, he cast a last glance around his bedroom wondering when and if he was going to see it again. He shook off the sadness, grabbed his luggage and phone, and off he went. He had to use the back door to make sure no one would see him. Luckily, they were all still in the living room, watching the *cat* fight.

As he stepped outside, he breathed in the fresh air of the night and let out a relieved sigh. *This is it*, he thought to himself as he glanced up and down the deserted street. This was the beginning of a new life. A life lived no more in his brother's shadow. A life where he would no longer be told what to do. He would be taking charge of everything in his life from now on.

Brandon made his way to to Clinton Avenue where he could find transportation. He didn't want to call a cab to the house because he knew it could easily be traced and he didn't know if Malik had that kind of pull. It was better to be safe than sorry.

As he waited for the bus, he basked in his freedom. It was intoxicating, filling him up and making him dizzy with happiness. It almost felt like he could grow wings at any moment and just fly away to wherever he wanted to go. If felt good to be free.

Right on schedule, the bus stopped in front of the sign and a heavy set toothless old driver opened the door for him. He paid for his ticket and carried his luggage over to a seat at the back of the bus. The bus was practically empty except for himself, the driver and another passenger who was leaning to the side passed out. He could tell the man was drunk because the smell of alcohol was strong as he moved by.

Brandon was drunk too. He was drunk on his newly acquired freedom. Leaving home was the first choice that he'd made on his own and he couldn't get enough of the feeling of independence.

It took two and an a half hours to reach his destination at 40 Washington Square in downtown Manhattan. He thanked the driver and got off in front of the entrance of the building holding a duffle bag in each hand. A feeling of belonging washed through him, putting him at ease.

Glancing up at the brick archway, he felt that once he crossed under, it would somehow confirm everything he had planned for himself. He looked over at the words on a small sign tarnished from weathering the years since 1835 and smiled.

New York University School of Law.

No one had known that he had applied for scholarships at several universities and had gotten accepted at more than four with full scholarships that included campus stay and meal tickets. Loving the vibe he'd gotten from the staff and the hum of energy he felt from the people that lived here in Greenwich Village, he knew this school was the perfect choice.

Not only was he close enough to visit his mother whenever he chose to, but he would still be able to keep an eye on Malik, documenting everything that he did. It wouldn't be long before he had a thick file on all his workers, trap houses, clients and connects. He would keep the information tucked safely away until he was ready to use it.

Brandon's plan was to study criminal law while acquiring the college credits he needed to apply for the police academy. Once he graduated from the police academy, he would begin to make his move on Malik's territory.

He would start out small arresting the corner hustlers. That would impress his lieutenant. Then he would start bringing down some of the more important members of his brother's organization, proving he was a good candidate for the Gang and Drug Enforcement.

As soon as he got his promotion, he would start running down on Malik's trap houses and everything, destroying Malik's so called dynasty. He was going to take it or destroy it all. *It would be like taking candy from a baby*, he thought with a smirk as he finally stepped through the gated archway.

CHAPTER 7

"We got two of them in the building and another two waiting outside," the man in the dark blue trench coat spoke into a tiny microphone, well-hidden among the buttons. He stood beside Brandon awaiting orders.

"Should I go in?" asked Brandon.

"Wait until they all get in," a sharp voice sounded in Brandon's ear. "It's a small house. They're gonna be caught in there like mice in a trap," replied his Sergeant.

"Roger that," Brandon mumbled with impatience.

The Sergeant could feel his officer's hatred burning through his ear, shooting to his brain like electricity. On one side, he could understand where that came from, but at the same time he kind of... didn't. Sure, like every decent human being around, he hated drug dealers for ruining people's lives. But on the other side, Brandon seemed to be the only one who did it with such a forceful passion.

Ever since he started working for the police department – and mind you, it had been a few good years – he hadn't met a man that wanted to do everything humanly possible to catch the drug dealers quite like him. Brandon Baker was an unstoppable force. A tireless machine that didn't fear even the most dangerous hustlas.

He had been on the force for a few years now, but was basically still a newbie. However, seeing how things were progressing with him, it wouldn't be a surprise to anyone if he was promoted.

The Sergeant cast another frugal glance to the house's entrance. The men were gone. They were most likely all inside and therefore, they made easy targets.

"They're in," he announced through the mic. Move in!"

Those were just the words Brandon had been waiting for. Armed to the teeth and followed by two other policemen, he busted through the house door.

"Police! Don't move!"

There were four men in front of Brandon, all looking about as dangerous as an old sock. Small time wannabe thugs, he concluded. And if he needed further proof, the little white plastic bags on the table came to his aid. It wasn't even a quarter of what an actual dealer would work with. But he had to deal with that for now. Plus, there was also a nice pile of dollar bills next to the bags that almost begged him to take it.

"Hands where I can see them!" he shouted as one of the men began reaching for his pocket. The move didn't go unnoticed by the other policemen because in the next second, the thug was saying hello to the floor, his nose pressed tightly against it as the officer checked his pockets. He took out a small revolver and tossed it to Brandon.

He caught the gun and started laughing.

"Is this what you guys use for defense? This pussy toy gun?"

"Fuck you think you are, nigga?" one of the thugs spat, casting Brandon a hatred-filled glance.

"If I were you, I'd watch my language," he replied sweetly, circling the small gun around his index finger. "You wouldn't want that dirty mouth getting you into trouble now, would you?"

"We got people everywhere, motherfucker," the man continued, prompting satisfied grins from the other thugs. "We gonna be outta there in no time and we'll come for yo bitch ass."

Boom!

As the man fell to the floor, the hole in his head getting bloodier by the second, Brandon blew the smoke that drifted above the gun's barrel. No one seemed to react.

"I hate them big-mouthed fools," he sighed. "Why can't y'all be nice and shut the fuck up once in a while? Let's get these pieces of shit outta here," he spoke as he took the money and drugs off the table and shoved them into a backpack he found nearby. "We gonna keep the greens, boys."

"What's going on in there?" asked the Sergeant from outside.

"We have three perps and one casualty. He went for his weapon and officer Baker fired in self defense. It was a clean shooting sir," said the officer.

"Good. Clean it up and clear out. I'm sending in forensic."

"Roger that."

None of the thugs said a word. They didn't even protest when the policemen cuffed them and forced them outside the house and inside the police car. Something told Brandon that it wasn't their first time seeing the inside of one.

Brandon slid behind the wheel of his car and radioed in to headquarters. Afterwards, he turned to look through the bullet proof plastic separating him from the thugs.

"Boys," he grinned as he gripped the wheel tightly. "You're in for a nice holiday in prison."

It had been Brandon's 19th catch. The 19th step to ruining his brother. And so far, he had never failed in putting criminal scum behind bars. It had become a hobby. Some sort of weird addiction that he couldn't, nor did he want to, give up. And that was just the beginning.

~~~~

Malik was seething. As he flipped aimlessly through the pages of a Motor magazine he could feel the blood boiling in his veins. He looked at the small man in front of him and felt his anger rising. He never liked Ibn. He only brought bad news whenever he'd pass by and even though he appreciated it, he'd reached a point where he saw him as a bad omen. This day was no exception.

"Where they holding them at?"

"Mac's place," Ibn replied, lighting himself a cigarette. He took a long drag from it and released it slowly. The smoke rose up like a silken thread twirling around in dance. It had a sour smell that Malik couldn't stand and he frowned. He had always hated cheap tobacco. "They got three of them and my man at the precinct tells me they ain't gonna let them go that easy."

"Three?" Malik asked, knowing he always had four guys to every house.

"Yeah, three. D-Man got popped."

"Fuck!" Malik said his anger rising. "And what the fuck you talking about they won't let them go?" Malik hissed through gritted teeth. "I pay Sam to make sure all my people are released after a night there!"

"Apparently, there's a new nigga in town meddling with our business," Ibn told him. "You think those three pieces of shit would've got caught otherwise? You know ain't nobody gonna bother with your operation."

"But this Mutha Fucker did."

"Yeah, dats facts. Never thought I'd live to see a clean cop," Ibn snorted.

"You know who he is?" Malik asked, his patience wearing thin. Three of his rookie men had been arrested and were at risk of never seeing the streets again for some small time shit, and this ugly motherfucker was standing in front of him smoking and joking like shit funny.

"I ain't got nothing yet," Ibn shrugged. "Sam told me he works in a different precinct. So he don't know him. There's a few noobs there anyway, so it's hard to tell who's who. But don't worry, man," he hurried to add when he saw Malik's savage look. "I'm working on that."

"You'd better fuckin' work faster," said Malik, his tone oddly calm. "Or else I'll fuckin' blow your brains out."

Ibn forced a laugh even though he was a little shook.

"I'll take care of everything, Malik. Don't worry about it." He got up and pressed the cigarette against the ashtray's cold glass until it went out. It wasn't even halfway smoked. "It's my business on the line too. This shit affects everybody."

Malik gave him a sharp look, still frowning.

After saying that, Ibn left the room, leaving Malik alone with his thoughts. He thought about this new guy and how he had to be fast and quiet in eliminating him. He couldn't let even the smallest disrespect go without retaliation. That's when motherfuckers start believing you're weak and try to take what you have.

He leaned back in his seat, knowing he had to hurry and deal with this new cop to set things straight again. He thought about his brother who was probably in some other state, working his ass off and catching criminals one by one. He smiled. If that was true, then it meant Brandon was the only one who made their father proud and in all honesty, he couldn't be happier knowing that he was the one that helped Brandon get where he was.

He decided to pass by his mother's house a bit later and maybe take her out for dinner. God knew when was the last time he'd taken her out.

~~~~

It was a cool summer evening and Brandon had one person on his mind, Bentley Mack. He heard from an insider that he was one of the few men who actually got to approach Malik without the risk of getting shot. And that was exactly the type of man he needed. The ones that were like vital arteries to his brother. The more he cut, the more he'd bleed. Only God knew how much he wanted to drain him dry.

This has been the second week he'd been watching Bentley. It took him a while to learn his habits, but he eventually managed to do it. Every Thursday at the exact same hour, he'd go to the same dirt cheap strip club, find exactly the same hooker, and pay her five hundred for a private dance and fuck. They both knew it was illegal and while one lived for that thrill knowing he wouldn't get caught, the other only saw it as yet another pay day.

"When's he comin' out?" his partner, Curtis, asked. "I'm getting' bored as hell sitting here."

Brandon didn't reply immediately. Instead, he checked his watch and with a smirk, he turned to the other man.

"He should be there right…now," said Brandon smiling.

The club's red door opened and out walked a tall, muscular man looking really relaxed. His belt was still unbuckled and his tie undone. It seemed that the usually punctual Bentley spent more time in there than he had planned.

They both waited patiently for Bentley to pass through the area where the lights didn't work, and when he finally did, they started their attack. The poor guy didn't even see where it came from. With a short blow to the temple, he was on the ground squirming in pain as the two men's pointy shoes dug into his flesh again and again.

"Stop!" he yelled, covering his face from an incoming hit.

They didn't say a word. If anything, their attack increased in intensity. Their hits got faster and harder until he couldn't even muster the strength to cover his face anymore. Brandon kneeled down in front of him, making sure the man couldn't distinguish his features and grabbed him by the collar.

"We know what you did, Bentley," he growled, emphasizing every word with a fist to the man's face. He didn't stop until his knuckles were soaked in blood. "We know you sell bad shit to good people and we're here to teach ya a lesson." Looking up at Curtis, he ordered, "Search his car. Leave the keys, but take everything else you can find. I'll search his clothes."

Curtis didn't wait to be told twice. He hurried to the car and

Brandon knew when he got there thanks to the distinct sound of glass breaking. Without saying any other word, he started doing what he had assigned himself. The man was too senseless to even think about protesting, so his job was a lot easier than his partner's. He only found a couple hundred dollars and a joint.

He took both.

"I know who you work for," he whispered in the man's ear. "Tell him that this is just the beginning."

He threw Bentley back on the ground and turned to leave, but not before spitting on him. He had never felt more powerful. He thought about the joint in his pocket and realized he didn't actually need that to get high. Power was all he needed to feel elevated.

"How much did ya get?" Curtis asked when he finally got in the car.

"Two hundred bucks and this bad boy," he replied, handing the joint to his partner. "Take it. I ain't got no need for that shit."

"You sure, though?"

"Of course. How much did ya get?"

Curtis smirked.

"The nigga had four thousand under his seat. We got rich tonight."

"We sure did," Brandon laughed. "Fucker stood no chance anyway."

"Which kinda surprised me, to be honest."

"Not really," he spoke, counting the money Curtis brought. "He was drunk as fuck. He was bound to have a date with that pavement sooner or later."

CHAPTER 8

Everybody was gathered in the conference room. Rookies, veterans and even some of the people who used to work there. No one told them what they were there for but one thing was certain — they were going to celebrate something. Or someone.

The general murmur stopped the second Sergeant Hardy entered the room, closing the door behind him. He didn't seem mad which was a good thing. Nobody wanted to have their ass chewed out first thing in the morning.

"I think we all know why we're here today," he spoke, fixing his blue silken tie, a gift from his wife that he was never seen without. It was an ongoing joke around the precinct that it was the only tie he owned.

"Not a clue," a man's voice came from the crowd, prompting amused chuckles from the others.

Sergeant Hardy smiled.

"We're here to congratulate our fellow crime fighter," he said as he pointed to Brandon, who was standing beside the window, a satisfied smile on his handsome face. He had known from the beginning why they were all there, of course. But he didn't want to ruin the surprise. He had already been congratulated about his arrest sheet yesterday.

"Brandon Baker, who single-handedly reduced the drug dealers' activity in our city by 5%."

As the first sounds of applause could be heard, the sergeant continued.

"After having discussed it with my superiors, we all agreed to make him the head of a new Special Drug Enforcement Unit."

The applause got louder and Brandon was basking in his colleagues' admiration. If only his Mom could see him at that exact moment. She would've regretted the day she picked Malik as the favorite son. She would look at him and see that it was he who deserved her appreciation and affection. Not some dirty drug dealer.

But soon Brandon wouldn't need to worry about Malik anymore. Once he was done tearing down his business, he would be the one his mother would be looking up to. Then he could see what it felt like to be second best.

What would remain of Malik? Just a memory. A sad, pathetic memory that he will sometimes think about when he'd be at the peak of success.

"Alright, alright," Sergeant Hardy shouted, quieting the room. "It's time we all got back to work. The criminals aren't going to catch themselves. Brandon, come with me. Your team is waiting for you in conference room B."

Brandon followed Sergeant Hardy from the room, his heart beating so fast he was afraid it might come out of his chest. He felt just like a kid on Christmas day.

In the conference room, the men were already waiting for him and they looked like nothing he had expected. They all had that fresh out of jail look. That spiteful gleam in their eyes and slight snarl on their lips that would frighten even the toughest thug. They looked like a bunch of hungry wolves. *Just what I need.*

"I know I said you could pick the guys that you wanted on your team, but are you sure about these guys? I mean most of them have been in trouble with the IA for using excessive force and none of them take orders well," said the sergeant.

Brandon had chosen these men for his own purposes. They all were having financial difficulties, were accused of taking bribes or they just plain hated dealers. Either way they would be extremely useful to him.

"No, they are exactly the type of men I need, sir. To be honest, I need men that aren't afraid of what's waiting for us out there. These guys have experience working in dangerous areas and that's exactly why I chose them. I need some hard hitting son of bitches that are willing to put it all on the line."

Sergeant Hardy chuckled. "Well, you've definitely picked the right bunch then," he said, shoving open the conference room door. "Say hello to your new team," he said, then walked away.

Brandon stepped into the room giving each man his scrutiny. They stared at him hard, but he returned their stares with just as much bravado. These men may look like they're the worst of the worst, but they were good men. They had families that they loved and put their lives on the line for every single day so they can feel a little safer.

Brandon gave the men a small nod as he moved to stand near the front of the room. "I'm Brandon Baker and I'll be directing this unit. Before we hit the streets and start to knock heads, how about some introductions?"

The guy closest to Brandon spoke up first. "Zane Hitchens." He was a white guy with an almost bald hair cut. His neck was super thick and he wore a pair of black framed glasses that belied his killer instinct. He rocked a tribal tattoo on the side of his neck that disappeared beneath his shirt. "I'm ready to rock and roll," he said with a sinister grin.

"I'm Brock Michaels," one of the two black men said. His eyes were dark and hard, yet bright with anticipation. Brock had curly hair that was growing into an afro and chiseled facial features. "I'm just here to put as many of these assholes away as possible."

Brandon nodded. "That's what I wanna hear."

"Chris O'Malley," a man with bright red hair said loudly, a slight grin on his face. "I've been shot twice, and dragged into the IA's office more times than I can count. What can I say? If you break the law, I'm gonna break your ass."

That prompted a few laughs from the guys.

The last two, another African-American man and a Russian thug were swift. They didn't give any back story and only told them their names – Devon DeMamp and Vladimir Fedorov.

"Alright. It's like this. You follow me and do as I say and we'll all reap the benefits. Understood?" asked Brandon, after all the introductions were over. When they all nodded, he continued.

He walked over to the white board and flipped it over revealing an outline of thugs and all their criminal activity. Each photo led up to a blank space at the top with no name.

"Our objective is to apprehend every person on this board until we find out who's running the whole operation. When we find out who's the head of the snake, we chop it off."

"Where do we start," asked Devon. The man stood almost six four with broad shoulders. He had a jagged scar across his jaw that enhanced his no nonsense demeanor.

"I got a tip from one of my insiders that there might be a pretty important gathering tomorrow on the East side. They're gonna be doing some business with the Mexicans. I hear it might be about forty grand in product being moved. That's twenty grand six ways if you get my meaning."

"I thought you said it would be forty grand down there," said Vladimir.

Brandon remembered reading that he was in jeopardy of losing his house.

"Yeah, it will be, but we have to turn in something or the Sergeant will begin to wonder what kind of deal these guys are down there making with no money. So we take half and turn in the rest. Got it?"

The men nodded their heads as they began to understand his method. Seeing the hungry look in their eyes showed him know he had been right in choosing them.

Malik, your days are numbered.

~~~~

"I wonder why your brother never joins us for dinner," Gloria sighed, circling the spoon in her soup bowl for the thousandth time. "He always seems to be too busy for us nowadays."

"Don't worry, Ma," Malik smiled, trying to reassure her. "He's making a name for himself. He'll come home soon."

Gloria took a sip of her soup and smacked her lips in satisfaction.

"Mmmm. This is the best thing you've ever cooked, boy. When did you learn to cook like this?" she said joking.

Malik shrugged, with a nonchalant expression. "Come on now. You know I get's down in the kitchen, Ma."

"Boy, everything you do in that kitchen you learned from me, so cut it out," she said laughing.

"Yeah, whatever. Besides, since I live alone, I have to cook. I gotta eat, right?" said Malik smiling. He shoved a large buttered roll into his mouth and washed it down with his mother's sweet tea.

"But what about that girl you were with last week?"

"Lucy?" he snorted. "She was only in it for the money. Plus, you know I can't get myself into anything serious cause of what I do."

There was a sudden moment of silence between them and it never felt more suffocating to Malik. He knew his mother didn't approve of what he did and she never brought it up. That is until lately. She's been questioning him about getting out of the game and even though he knows she is right, he always made an excuse about it not being the right time.

Afterwards, he would feel weighted down about his guilt. It always felt like he was being pushed under a mountain and forced to carry it. Were those his sins that he'd committed crawling on his back? Was that his father's disappointment he felt stinging his heart with such force? He knew it to be the truth, which is why he had stopped going to his grave site to visit him. *I let him down big time.*

"I never agreed to this, you know," she finally spoke, her voice soft and her eyes glistening with the tears she had been fighting to keep at bay. "Every day I just sit here and wonder if today will be the day that I'll never see you again. I hope and pray that you won't get into a fight and get hurt or that the police won't get to you." She paused for a second and sighed. "I like to think I'm a fair woman and I respect the law, but now I'm rooting for a..."

He knew exactly what his mother was going to say. And he also knew how hard it was for her to live with the fact that she had raised a criminal. *I even let her down.*

Malik dropped his head low, his chin damn near hitting his chest. No one knew that sometimes he felt ashamed of what he had become. He knew he sacrificed his future to take care of his family, but the true question he kept asking himself is *Who are you doing it for now?*

He glanced over in his mother's direction and saw the tear slide down her face.

"If it makes you feel any better, I tried looking for an actual job after Brandon left for school. But my name drew too much attention. People are scared of me, Ma. They don't want to be around a drug dealer and I understand that. I didn't even get upset about it."

Gloria nodded in acceptance. She reached up and placed her hand on the side of his face. He looked so much like his father that it was sometimes hard to see him.

"I understand baby, but try and think of something else you can do. Maybe you can open up your own business. You're smart and people respect you."

"Some do, but most fear me. There's a difference." When he saw her shoulders drop he knew she was feeling worse. "But I will give it some thought. Maybe opening a few stores or something is a good idea."

Gloria smiled. "Yeah, and if you need any help with anything I'll be there."

"I can't pay you though," he said smiling.

Gloria elbowed him playfully. "Boy, stop. Eat your food before it gets cold."

Malik smiled, thankful that their conversation hadn't spoiled the evening. But for Gloria, it still didn't mean she was okay with the outcome of that discussion. She was still hoping that he would give up that dangerous lifestyle and settle down with a nice woman and find a legal way of making money.

~~~~

Brandon smirked and felt a shiver of excitement flow through him. *This was going to be one hell of a productive day*, he thought as he looked at the whiteboard in his office. He had arrived early that morning, eager to start chasing down the suspects.

"Morning," O'Malley said as he stepped in the room. He was carrying a black backpack that made a loud clanking sound when he tossed it on the chair. "I don't work like y'all," he explained when he saw Brandon's puzzled look. "I use these bad boys."

He unzipped the backpack and withdrew a rolled up tarp. When he untied it Brandon saw that it was filled with a few deadly looking knives. O'Malley pulled one free of its sheath and flipped it around, always catching the handle.

Shiny and horrifyingly sharp, their sight gave Brandon goose bumps. It was a weird mix of excitement and fear, and he loved it. He could barely wait until they started.

"What are you going to use when you run out of knives," asked Brandon.

O'Mally smiled wickedly and opened his jacket showing two shiny guns at his side. "Oh, I still have my two best friends."

Brandon laughed and shook his head.

"When are the rest of the guys gonna show up?" O'Malley asked, placing the knife back into place and shoving them back in his backpack. "I'm ready to get this done and have a beer, shit."

"They'll be here in a bit," Brandon said, a slight tinge of malice on his lips as he pulled his own gun from its holster and checked the clip again. "But I'm glad you're so excited."

One by one, the members of his team entered the room, each of them looking dangerous and intimidating. Brandon couldn't help a small chuckle. It was the perfect team. These men were hungry for the kill and using their badge as an explanation for it. In the streets, most of them would be considered criminals, but when you have the badge behind you, its legal. You're just doing your job.

After assessing all the details, they followed Brandon outside where two black trucks with tinted windows were waiting for them. He hopped in the first one, followed by the Russian and his semi-automatic rifle, a dark SKS that had the man's initials painted on it in red ink.

Devon slid into the back seat, quiet as usual. O'Malley, Zane and Brock piled in the second truck. They were all fully armed with bullet proof vest and small ear plugs.

"First stop, Macy's Club," Brandon announced as he drove off.

The men knew exactly what that club was and not surprisingly, they were quite eager to get there. It was an old strip club that only functioned as a cover for what was actually going on there.

Heroin addicts, and dealers alike, always gathered there to do business. The club had always been one of Brandon's main targets, but because he didn't have the right team backing him up, he could never actually take measures against it. Today was different.

They all stepped inside and headed towards a table in the back. They were aware that they looked suspicious and that several men were watching them, but they couldn't care less. They all knew, thanks to Brandon, what was actually going on there and wouldn't hesitate to burn the place down if given the order.

But Brandon had other ideas. He knew that it would've been a loss of precious space. Space that would be used for better purposes in the future. His future. So any thought of destroying it was out. He was there for one particular person and he'd just walked in.

Paul Rudd slammed the main door open, demanding an entire bottle of vodka once he reached the counter. The bartender complied and when he finally saw the bottle of clear liquor in front of him, he started drinking desperately. He was putting away the vodka like a man who had been lost in the desert for years.

"Your liver's gonna fail you one day, Paul," Brandon spoke as he approached the man and pushed the bottle away.

"Look who's here," the man spoke, his tone obviously mocking. "Lil' Brannie, the hustlas' arch enemy. I'm guessing you're here to arrest me?"

"Not really," Brandon smirked. He lifted the bottle of vodka and let his lips caress the bottle's opening. "You'll be lucky if you get out of here alive."

Paul burst into laughter. It was a hyena-like bark to the smoke impregnated ceiling.

"Ya think a lil' city cop like you has the power to take me down? How fucking naïve of ya."

At a sign from Paul, Brandon was surrounded by a few dangerous looking thugs. They had been lurking in the shadows, waiting for their boss' signal. Hell, some of them weren't even hired by him. They were small time wannabes hanging around the place hoping for a chance to be down.

Paul laughed. "What you need to do is stop trying to be like ya brother. You ain't got it in you kid," he said, reaching for the vodka.

Suddenly, a single shot rang out. Boom! One of Paul's thugs was lying on the floor, a small puddle of blood already forming under his head. Paul looked down at him in shock. Brandon hadn't moved, so who the hell had shot one of his boys. He never got the chance to find out.

Brandon took that first shot as a signal. With a swift movement, he pulled out his own gun and shot Paul straight between the eyes. He took a few more thug's lives before a sharp pain shot through his head. His body dropped to the floor, and the last thing he saw was Paul's lifeless body lying next to him.

~~~~

After the incident at Macy's Bar, Brandon told himself that he'd have to be more cautious around seemingly unarmed thugs. He had a pretty big scar on his temple to make sure he would never forget his foolish mistake. Luckily, his doctor said it would heal up nicely.

He had been in the hospital for a few days and needed several stitches to fix the ugly wound a man's knife had left. But that had been only a small hurdle. He had unfinished business at Macy's Club.

At one point he'd wanted to leave the club untouched, but now the thought of that place left a bad taste in his mouth. The first thing he did after getting out of the hospital was to go back to the club and empty it of everyone inside. He then poured gasoline everywhere and with a blank expression of indifference, he tossed a match inside.

The club went up in flames consuming the whole building almost instantly. The fire destroyed everything; the liquor, tables and more importantly, the heroin stashed in the basement. It wasn't long before the local news stations picked up the story airing it on the evening news.

However, just like any other story that involved the police, it was quickly covered up. No one came forward to give a statement about that night at the club and no one claimed responsibility for setting the fire. All the public knew was that a place known for selling drugs and prostitution was finally wiped from their neighborhood.

Brandon felt good. For now, he was above the law.

CHAPTER 9

Little by little, Malik's empire was falling apart. Group after group, dealer after dealer, they all fell prey to Brandon's anger. He felt that things couldn't get any better. He got to take down the most dangerous drug dealers around, in the most brutal ways he could imagine, and he couldn't get punished for it. Instead, he was basking in the adoration of his co-workers and superiors.

That was just a small bonus for him, though. His true reward will come the moment he had completely gotten rid of every hustla associated with Malik. Only after that, would he go to his mother and tell her everything he'd done. Well, not all the details, of course, but he would make sure she would see him as the hero he actually was. *Way better than a dirty drug dealer.*

And where would that leave Malik? Rotting in a small jail cell, wondering where it all went wrong.

He took a sip of his coffee, smacking his lips and frowning at the taste. It was some shitty corner store coffee O'Malley bought. But shit, to him, even the shitty coffee wasn't enough to dampen his mood.

"You got the house monitored?" Brandon asked O'Malley when he sat down on the sofa in the office.

"Of course, mate," he nodded, swirling his cup of coffee around carefully. "Vladimir's been there since last night. He said those assholes have been there all night, drinking and smoking."

Brandon snorted. "As if they would've been doing anything productive."

O'Malley opened his mouth to reply, but was quickly cut off by the sound of the slamming door. Zane came in stomping his heavy boots on the floor. He looked angry.

"What's the matter?" asked Brandon.

He didn't speak right away. With shaking hands, he took a glass off the table and filled it with water. After gulping it all down, he let himself fall on the sofa and finally uttered, "I think someone snitched on us."

"What the fuck you mean?" Brandon inquired, his eyes widening in disbelief. No one knew about their missions except the small task force group and their superior.

"They moved. They took everything from that house and ran away as if they were being chased by fuckin' demons. Someone snitched, I'm telling you. I bet it was that fucker, Brock. He looked hella shady from the beginning."

"Let's not jump to conclusions now," Brandon told him, his tone calm and calculated. "I'll go ask around and see if someone else from the department is to blame for this shit."

Zane and O'Malley waited for his return in an uncomfortable silence. They didn't really enjoy each other's company, so no words were spoken. They moved around the room, both wondering who the snitch could be.

It took Brandon half an hour and a few threats to the right people until he eventually found out that a small team of newbies had found out about his plan to raid the drug house and craving some recognition, decided it would be a great idea to take the task upon themselves. It didn't go well, as expected. Two of the young cops were dead, another one was injured and the gang had moved to another location.

Thankfully, Brandon still had Vladimir surveying them. He had noticed something fishy about the whole operation and decided to act on his own and keep following them. They were currently settled in a smaller house, right next to the cinema.

It had been a great plan, Brandon thought. They thought it would be safe to move to a more populated area where the police couldn't land any brutal assaults. *But I couldn't care less about the casualties,* Brandon thought, a malicious grin slid across his face.

"Alright," he said when he returned back to his office. "It was some rookie bullshit, but it's fixed now. Just talked to Vladimir and he gave me the address of their new location. So grab your shit and let's go cut up some niggas."

~~~~

The place was quiet. Almost too quiet, if you asked Brandon. Were the thugs waiting for them?

He signaled to his team to wait a bit longer until he figured out what was going on. Oddly enough, the house itself didn't look like a place where some of the most dangerous criminals would gather for business. It was small and white, with a red door and a big porch swing. His mother would've loved it.

Suddenly, a light came on and he could clearly see one of the inhabitants, an elderly man, putting on his oven mitts and disappearing under the window frame for a brief moment. *Probably taking out something from the oven*, Brandon thought.

"What the fuck's happening in there?" O'Malley asked, narrowing his eyes at the odd sight in front of him.

"You sure this is the right place?"

Brandon didn't reply. Instead, he whispered an order in his microphone and left the guys alone while he started circling the house. Nothing seemed odd or out of place, but he trusted Vladimir's word, so he kept searching for the smallest thing that could've given away the thugs hideout. The Russian swore he saw them entering the house and yet, they were nowhere to be found. He made a mental note to ask for a few K9 dogs.

"… and this is where she hit me, the fucking whore. Right in the gut."

Brandon's ears perked up at the sound of the unknown voices. From what he could make out, it belonged to a man not older than thirty. It was so raspy and deep that he probably smoked a few blunts a day.

He heard laughter and as he got closer to the back of the house, the voices became louder and clearer. It was odd. All the rooms were dark and empty, yet…

Just then, a strong gust of wind hit him in the face, forcing him to close his eyes so he wouldn't get blinded by the dust. When he lowered his head to shield his eyes, he couldn't help but grin. The weather was apparently rooting for him that night because the wind had blown off some leaves of what seemed to be a trap door leading under the house.

A basement! He could barely contain his excitement as he went back to his team and dictated the instructions. He had a very detailed plan made up. If they worked as a team, everyone would get to go home tonight.

"Zane and O'malley, you two go inside and make sure whoever is in there won't warn the others. Vlad, you stay here and keep the house under surveillance. Brock and Deven, you two come with me. We're gonna catch the rats in their nest," he said grinning wickedly.

He was glad to see that they had similar grins on their faces. They seemed to be just as eager that night as he was. He didn't ask or care why. As long as they wanted the same thing, he was satisfied. "Cover up," he said through his microphone, and they all pulled black ski masks over their faces.

The success of the mission would mean his brother's empire would take a heavy blow. Six of his most trusted men were in that basement at the moment, all awaiting their deaths. Brandon's muscles flexed with anticipation. He couldn't wait to bring these fools down.

They didn't hurry. They walked slowly, their steps light and calculated. They knew that the smallest sound would alert the people inside and their whole mission would be ruined. Brandon was also pleased to notice that the house was quiet as well. That meant that the men he sent inside did their jobs perfectly.

When they reached the trapdoor, he signaled to his men to get their guns ready. When the last reloading click was heard, he moved into position.

"Here's Johnny!" he growled as he shot the lock, and kicked the door open with his foot.

He was welcomed by a small round of bullets, but he had been prepared for that. With the thick riot shield protecting his face, he quickly moved to the side near a large brick wall. He wore his bullet proof vest under his uniform and felt comfortable about leaving his cover spot. He lifted his gun and began to return fire.

After the initial shock had vanished, the thugs realized there was no way they could escape. The main exit up the steps was blocked by O'Malley, while the trap door had been seized by Brandon and the rest of his men.

O'Malley saw a Chinese guy with a blonde mohawk pointing his gun at Devon and fired a bullet straight through his forehead. Brandon recognized him as Mr. White, the main crack dealer on the east side. It was said he was the first to bring drugs in that area and for that, he had the others' respect. Apparently, he had been working for Malik as well.

After the second round of shots was fired from the enemy squad and barely missing Brock right shoulder, Brandon decided it was time to move forward with his plan.

"Whoa, man. Hold your fire. We came to talk," he yelled.

"The fuck do you want, nigga?" one of the thugs snapped at him, his gun pointed in Brandon's direction. He recognized the man as Mort, the heroin addict and dealer. He was blind in one eye, yet it didn't make him a weak link. He was one of the worst in Malik's group.

However, he wasn't a match for Brandon and his men. He had to give it to him, though. His courage was foolishly admirable.

"We wanna collab," Brandon spoke, enjoying the distrustful reactions his words got from the drug dealers.

"By force?" Mort asked, his eyes narrowing in rage.

"By any means," Brandon smirked.

He gave a small hand signal that had his men form into a tight ball. With his team protected behind his shield, and wearing their heavy vests, the hustlas didn't stand a chance. One by one, all five remaining men were taken down, their blood mixing together into a giant dark stain. It was a grim reminder that if you messed with him, you were going to end up with your brains scattered on the floor.

After the last man fell, Brandon sat down at the table and gulped down a half finished glass of brandy.

"We should celebrate, guys," he smiled, pointing at the stack of cash on the table. "We're killing scum and getting rich doing it."

"Amen to that!" said Zane. He took the bottle of alcohol and gulped down a few swallows.

O'Malley didn't seem to understand what was happening.

"So what are we gonna do with this?" he asked, pointing at the money.

Brandon burst into laughter.

"It's ours. We found it, we keep it. What was the deal with the old man upstairs?"

"He was the uncle of one of these fuckers," O'Malley replied, casting a disgusted look at the dead bodies on the floor. "I don't think he knew what was going on to be honest. He seemed scared when we first got into the house, but gladly gave us all the answers we needed."

"So he was scared," Brandon said.

"Yup. But not because of us. He was afraid of his nephew."

A slight pang of sadness shot through Brandon's heart. He felt bad for the old man. He probably was trying to live a peaceful life, but was being assaulted by his nephew and his gang of criminal friends.

"Alright, let's clean this shit up," he ordered, looking for his backpack. He quickly shoved all the money inside, wondering how much they were going to rake after the split.

His thought's drifted to his mother thinking it wouldn't be long before he would be able to give her a few expensive gifts. He saw her hugging him and kissing his cheek with love and gratitude. He always had visions of how she would react to his generosity, and it always played out the same in all of them.

Brandon, the neglected son, would finally get all the love and affection he deserved from his mother. *It would feel good*, he thought. Then he looked down at the bag full of money. *But all this cash in my backpack feels way better.*

CHAPTER 10

"What the fuck, man? Are you actually leaving us on our own today?" Brock grumbled, clearly upset at the news he just heard.

"It's not like you can't handle a group of college niggas. Don't be stupid. Plus, I promised."

Brock's face showed nothing but discontent. Brandon was leaving town that Friday, so that meant they were on their own in this evening's raid. It was nothing complicated, as he insisted – just a few college kids thinking they could get into '*the business*.' But the main problem was that they didn't know who backed them up and that could create more trouble than they wanted.

"Do you at least have any useful information to give us?" Brock asked, lighting up another cigarette. Brandon scrunched his nose. He hated that cheap shit his men smoked.

"You know just as much as I do," came his stern reply. He was tired of this conversation already and yet, Brock didn't seem to be leaving.

"You're not lying, are ya?"

Brandon let out an exasperated groan.

"I told you already," he said, trying his absolute best to maintain the calmness in his tone. "Why the fuck would I keep info from you? You think I wanna get you all killed or some shit?"

"I never said that. I was just hoping there would be something you forgot."

"I don't see why you're so worried about this crap," Brandon sighed. "It's just a bunch of fuckin' freshmen thinking they're cool. You won't even need all the men for that. Actually, I think it's for the best if you only take one person with you."

"We don't know who's backing them, man!"

"Their fuckin' parents are backing them!" Brandon shouted, his fist colliding loudly with the desk in front of him. "Are you done being such a lil' bitch? I thought I got some ruthless mother fuckers on my team, not fuckin' cowards. Fuck!"

Brock didn't seem too impressed. He took another drag from his cigarette and watched the smoke rising up to the ceiling.

"I was just making sure this ain't nothing serious. A lot of shit has been happening lately and you can't always know who's who."

"This is nothing serious," Brandon said. "Now get the fuck out and let me get ready. And open the window before ya leave. That shit smells like rotting corpses."

Laughing, Brock did as he was told. There was no use in annoying Brandon anymore since it was obvious that he didn't know anything else.

A sigh escaped Brandons' lips as soon as he heard the click of the door being closed. Where did they even find these people? Each and every one of them stubborn as a mule and just as stupid as the next one. If they hadn't been hired by his superiors, he would've gotten rid of them a long time ago. Well, not exactly all of them, he thought. Just the dumbest ones. Maybe he could arrange some accident. He would think about it some other time.

For now, he had to get ready to go meet his mother.

He fixed his tie in the small mirror on his desk and made sure his hair looked impeccable before putting on his best suit coat. It's been a while since he had last seen his mother and he wanted to look perfect. She was definitely going to be impressed. And most of all, proud to have such a great son.

He could already see his brother in his sagging jeans and white t-shirt. Compared to him, Malik would look like a young high school gangster wannabe. He chuckled to himself.

In front of the precinct, a taxi stopped and after a few honks, Brandon remembered he had been the one who called for it. He grabbed his suitcase and flew out of the door.

He forgot one thing though, and that was exactly what Brock had been waiting for.

After making sure Brandon was gone for good, he crept into his office and started rummaging through his papers. What a lucky fuckin' day, he thought, pulling out a red file labeled "high risk." The dumb ass left both his office and drawers unlocked in his hurry to leave.

He knew some people who would pay good money for what was

in that file.

~~~~

Brandon always hated when complete strangers tried to make small talk. And he hated it even more when they didn't take the hints and started talking about every small thing that crossed their minds. Like the taxi driver.

For the past half an hour, Brandon learned that democrats had no chance in winning the elections that year, that Leo wasn't actually supposed to win the Oscar, and that the world will finally come to an end once the government finally started their evil plot of freezing the Earth to death by controlling the weather. At one point, he started thinking that jumping out of the car while it was speeding down the street wouldn't be such a bad idea.

"We're finally here, mister," the driver announced, pulling over in front of a small but nice-looking house. He grinned when he saw that Brandon had tipped him, showing off his golden tooth. "Lost it in a fight with an Italian mobster," he explained as if Brandon actually cared.

Not waiting for another word, Brandon slammed the car door closed and took a deep breath of relief when he was finally free of the talkative old fucker. He shook his head, regretting that he tipped that lunatic. *Whatever*, he shrugged. He was feeling extra generous that day.

He only needed to knock once before the door opened, his mother stood there, her face lit up by the brightest smile. *She looks even prettier than the last time I'd seen her*, he thought.

She was wearing a black dress with daisies on it and had her hair up in a bun. He was so happy to see her like that. She was radiating sheer happiness and that was more than enough to make him happy too.

"Hi, Mom," he said shyly. "It's good to s—"

Before he could finish, he was pulled into the warmest embrace he had ever felt.

"Come in, come in," his mother beamed, inviting him inside. "Oh, what a great day. To have both my sons home for dinner again!"

"Both?" he asked as his smile began to drift away.

She nodded.

"Your brother is coming in a bit. He said he has a surprise for me."

He could barely hold in a jeering snort. It came out as an odd sneeze instead. While he was busy pretending he was looking for a tissue, his mother took his coat and hung it on the mahogany clothes hanger. *Another gift from her beloved drug dealer son*, he thought. It took all the self control he could muster not to sound heated when he spoke. Instead, his tone came across as friendly, and sickly sweet.

"I can't wait to see him either. It's been a while."

Gloria nodded. "I know, I know. I'm pretty sure he'll love to see you here!"

Brandon followed her into the living room, passing by a set of modern art paintings. There was nothing to be admired there except the straightness of the lines that made the geometric shapes randomly thrown onto the canvas. *Waste of money.*

The living room had been redecorated as well. His eyes were drawn to a small glass table in the middle of the room resting on top of a white fur rug. *Probably real.*

There were a few chairs in the odd shape of a half moon, their feet pointy and black. The white walls were covered in white bookshelves packed with books he was pretty sure no one ever read.

"Do you like it?" his mother asked, her eyes glowing with pride. "I took care of all the decorating process!"

"With whose money?"

He regretted the words as soon as they left his lips. They hung heavy in the air between them, pressing on their shoulders like mountains. He snapped. He shouldn't have. *Not at her. Never at her.*

"With mine and Malik's, if you must know," she uttered through her teeth. "I work too, you know. I'm not lazy."

"I know, Ma. I know," he sighed, wrapping his arms around her. "I didn't mean it like that. I just..."

"It's alright. The trip must have tired you," she said, forcing a smile. "Why don't you take a nap? It's gonna take a while until everyone's here so you might as well rest."

Brandon looked at her closely and for the first time he noticed that his mother was getting old. Her brown eyes were still bright and she was still beautiful, however, she now had tiny wrinkles that were slowly becoming noticeable. The wrinkles around her mouth, the lines on her forehead, and even the few white hairs he thought were just a trick of the light, gave away what she'd gone through worrying about Malik. That made him feel even worse for what he'd said earlier, but angry at Malik for making her worry so much.

"You're right. I'm sorry I snapped like that. I just had an argument with a colleague before leaving and it kinda got to me."

She got on her toes, reaching for his cheek so she could kiss it. She laughed when he pretended to pull away.

"You know where your room is," she said releasing him. "It's still the same as you left it."

He nodded and went upstairs.

She was right. His room was still the same way it had been while he had been growing up in. The same bed, desk and chair. Even the posters of basketball players still hung on the walls. He ran his fingers on the glossy surface of one, remembering how he'd sometimes gazed at them and dreamed about becoming one of the famous NBA players. He liked to imagine himself on posters like that, being an inspiration for another kid like him.

He sat down at his desk and pulled open a drawer. His stuff was still there, untouched by the hands of time. He found a few pens, some Crayolas and a few old notebooks. He took one out and opened it, laughing at the doodles he'd drawn during math class. What an awesome time that had been. He had hated it then, just as every other child that was obligated to attend school. Now, when he recalled those days, he wished he could go back.

Those were the good times when it had just been himself, his mother and father, and Malik, who wasn't yet a filthy drug dealer. A flash of pain struck his heart. He wished everything was different. He wished his father was still alive so he could continue to give his *golden boy'* Malik all his attention. Then his mother would be free to continue to give him all of hers. He missed her praising him and being eager to hear about his day. *Now it was all about Malik.*

With a deep sigh, Brandon got up and flopped down on the twin bed. *I wish I didn't have to hunt down my own brother. But someone's gotta teach him a lesson.*

It was his last thought before he fell into a dreamless sleep.

~~~~

An hour later Brandon woke up to the sound of voices downstairs. One of them belonged to his mother, that he knew for sure. But there were two more he wasn't able to recognize. He figured out one must have been his brother's and yet there was still another one. A woman's voice he could not make out.

"Brandon!" his mother cheered as soon as he walked into the

kitchen. "There you are!"

"Hey, bro," Malik said, reaching out to shake Brandons' hand. "It's nice to see ya again."

Malik looked over his brother and felt a surge of pride at the man he'd become, knowing he had a hand in making it so.

Oh, it would be truly nice to see you when you're behind bars, he wanted to say. Instead, he put on the best fake smile he could and greeted his brother with warmth.

"Nice to see you too, bro," he said. "And who's that lovely lady over there?"

The girl flashed a bright smile. She was stunning. Her long wavy hair flowing over her chocolate shoulders in a silky cascade. Her big brown eyes glowing with pleasure. She had full lips and sculpted cheeks, giving her the arrogant air of a model.

"I'm Terry," she spoke, shaking Brandon's hand. He couldn't help but focus on the touch of her silky smooth skin. "Malik's girlfriend."

"I'm so lucky to have met her," Malik spoke, sheer pride dripping from his voice. "She's a goddess."

"Oh, stop," she giggled. "You're making me blush."

Gloria, obviously proud of her older son, couldn't stop fretting around him and his girlfriend. She kept repeating how beautiful Terry was and how proud she was of Malik. It shamed Brandon to admit it, but it kind of made him feel as if he was lacking something. As if he couldn't measure up.

"Okay, mom," Malik laughed.

"Yeah, yeah," Gloria said, slightly embarrassed. "It's not often one of my sons bring a woman home for dinner. That being said, I made a killer grilled rabbit."

"Skilled as always," Brandon said, placing a small kiss on his mother's cheek. He felt oddly proud of himself for having thought about that compliment before his brother.

They all took it upon themselves the task of helping with setting the dinner table. After the food had been arranged on the table and the good cutlery was taken out, they all sat down around the massive wooden table. Their mouths began to water at the delicious meal in front of them. When Malik reached for the first bite, his mother gently slapped his hand.

"You know we pray first in this house. Who should be the one to do it?"

"I think that should be you, Ma," Brandon said. "You're the host, after all. We'll just follow you."

She seemed happy with that. They all joined hands, Brandon caught between his mother and Terry, a spot he rather enjoyed.

"Lord almighty," she began and Brandon could feel how her grip on his hand got tighter. He could tell it was the same for his brother as well. "Please accept our humble prayers and thanks. I thank you for bringing my sons together this evening and for blessing us with Terry. I thank you for the life we have and I thank you for the food you put on our table. Amen."

"Amen," the others repeated.

"Can I eat now?" Malik asked, just as he used to when he was a child.

Gloria laughed and, much to his surprise, Brandon followed her.

"Of course."

They ate together, laughing and talking about the small things that made them either happy or annoyed. Long moments of laughter were often followed by short silent pauses when each of them would either focus on their food, either letting something sink in, be it a joke or a serious remark. It was Malik's turn to break the silence that time.

"So," he spoke, reaching for the gravy, "what do you do, bro? You never told us? I mean the way you left the night of your party, we didn't know what to think. We were happy you called and said you had decided to leave early for school. You never said what your major was, though."

That was just what Brandon had been expecting. An opportunity to brag about his super dangerous job. How he risked his life to keep the streets safe and how he made sure the young kids wouldn't follow any wrong path in life.

"I'm working as a cop at the moment," he said, enjoying the look on his mother's face. She looked impressed and that was everything that mattered at that moment. "Just a plain old cop," he continued, realizing it wouldn't be a good move on his side to reveal his actual occupation. "Patrolling the streets and making sure everybody's safe. Nothing interesting, really."

"Are you kidding me?" Malik said, a wide grin etched on his face. "That's amazing, man. Congratulations! I know Dad would've been so proud of you!"

"Yes, he would have," Gloria repeated. She didn't look sad and

Brandon was happy to see that she wasn't. Usually when his father's name was mentioned she'd get this mournful look and it pained him to see it. It seemed that she remembered only the happy memories now, rather than recalling that terrible day.

"What about you?" Brandon asked Malik, happy to see the smile fading from his face.

"Same old struggle," Malik shrugged, trying to look like it was nothing, but Brandon knew that it wasn't true.

His business wasn't going as smooth as it used to and he and his crew were the ones responsible for it. One thing that surprised him though, was the plain discontent that showed on Terry's face as soon as he'd mentioned it.

"But nevermind about that," Malik hurried to add, eager to change the subject. "You're a policeman, dude! I'm so proud of you. I have no words to describe how much!"

Brandon smiled. Of course he was proud of him. He was actually helpful to the society in a way. He, on the other hand, sold drugs on the corners of the street pulling the poor people in a vicious circle that would eventually ruin their lives.

Of course he was proud of him, when his only recognition in life was becoming the 'Drug King' as the hustlas called him.

Of course he was proud, when he couldn't even finish his studies cause he was too busy wasting poor people's money on tasteless expensive shit to impress their mother.

He laughed at him silently, mocking every word he said. He couldn't wait until he finally stripped him of everything he had. Then their mother would see him for what he truly was; an uneducated, broke and useless waste of time.

CHAPTER 11

"Alright, look," Brandon said. "I'll call ya later. I got a few hours to myself and I wanna go run a few errands. I'll see ya in a bit."

Without waiting for the other person to respond, he ended the call. He didn't like to hear anything work-related during his free time. It only stressed him out. Plus, it had been a relatively quiet period, as odd as that was. His crew could manage a few rebel teens on their own.

He headed out the door and quickly got into the back of a cab.

"Where you headed?" asked the driver.

"Head to Jersey Gardens Mall," replied Brandon.

"Here we go," said the driver as he merged into traffic.

Finally, after twenty long quiet minutes, they were there, and as usual the place was packed. There were mostly a bunch of kids there that were walking around waiting for their movie to start since the theatre was right next to the mall. Then there were the die hard shoppers, the deal catchers, the tourist, and the tired ass players that came to hit on women.

Taking out his earphones, Brandon searched for his favorite song while heading to the shoe store. There were many shoe stores in the mall, but his favorite was the small Italian one at the top floor. It always had the finest quality leather, not to mention all the cashiers had fat asses.

As he passed by a beauty salon, he felt a sudden tug on his sleeve. When he turned around, Terry was standing in front of him, a big smile on her face.

"Hey, Terry," he said as they hugged quickly. "What are you doing up here," he asked looking around. He expected Malik to step out any second.

She chuckled.

"I'm waiting my turn to get my hair done. I come here every week."

"Did you miss last weeks appointment?" he asked, teasing her.

"So funny," she grinned, gently punching his shoulder. "What are you doing here, though? Aren't you supposed to be catching bad guys?"

He shrugged. "I have this morning off. Nothing big was happening right now, so I left my people to deal with whatever may come."

"Oh, so you have subordinates?" she asked, seemingly impressed. "You forgot to mention that."

"I don't like to brag," he smiled, his gaze swerving along her generous curves. She wore a black tight dress and black heels that made her sexy legs look even longer. He decided the shoes could wait. "Are ya busy?" he asked. "I was thinking we could go for a coffee and get to know each other better," he said innocently.

"Not at all," came her reply. He was happy to see that she looked eager. "Should we go down to the cafeteria?"

He shook his head.

"Nah. I know a better place."

Half an hour later, they were sitting in a small café, laughing and enjoying the delicious coffee. It was a rather small place, but it made up for that in coziness. There weren't any actual chairs, only fluffy pillows and small tables that were low to the floor. The walls were covered in paintings of black and white landscapes. The people and the music – smooth jazz – made them feel like they were in heaven.

"So how's it going?" Brandon asked, pouring a bit of milk into his coffee.

"Pretty good," she replied, though unsure of her answer. "I mean my job and family are good."

"What about Malik?"

She looked away for a second and fortunately for her, her gaze met the waiter's and she ordered tea. It covered perfectly the awkward silence that would've followed.

"It's alright," she finally spoke, a tinge of irritation in her voice.

"Doesn't sound like it to me."

She sighed. "It's just—It's what he does, you know?"

Ah, so that was the problem. She couldn't cope with his so called job. And if anyone could understand that, it was him.

"Did he bring drugs home or something?" he asked, pushing her for an explanation.

"No. No, nothing like that!" she quickly answered, looking embarrassed. "I just think it's dangerous. I don't really feel safe anywhere. What if some random thug decides to piss him off by murdering me?"

"Have you talked to him about that?"

"I did once. He told me he would stop doing it after things got serious between us, but as you can see, he didn't keep that promise. Now I rarely even find time to talk to him. He just comes home once every three or four days and when he does, it's late at night when I'm already asleep."

He could see the sadness in her eyes. She looked so helpless and fragile in that moment. *How perfect*, he thought. Yet another weapon to be used against his brother. It was like the universe itself pieced this puzzle together in such a way that he would have the most advantage.

"Such a shame," he smiled, his lips caressing the edge of his cup as he took a sip of his coffee. "He has a real treasure next to him and he leaves it untouched."

Much to his satisfaction, the corners of her mouth curled into a small smile.

"I wouldn't really say treasure," she murmured, looking down, a slight tinge of red coloring her cheeks.

"Don't be modest," he chuckled. "Look at you. You're absolutely perfect. What man in his right mind wouldn't like to show you off to the world?"

"Your brother, I'm guessing," she said bitterly, with a half laugh.

"I'm not my brother," he told her, his hand reaching for hers. The attraction was almost instant. The second they looked into each other's eyes, they knew what was to come. And neither of them felt bad about it. On the contrary, they could barely wait.

"I'll book a room at the hotel for tonight," he murmured against her skin as he kissed her hand. "What do you say?"

She bit her lip, her eyes burning with desire. Malik hadn't touched her in weeks and her kitty was playing a Congo beat in her panties right now. Brandon was handsome with dark, ominous eyes, smooth brown skin and shoulders strong enough to lift a woman. *I need to be lifted.*

Without another thought she made her choice. "I say it's perfect."

"I'll call you when I'm done with work."

As they exchanged phone numbers, Brandon felt something stir inside him. It wasn't a pleasant feeling, as one might expect after a date with such a stunner. It felt uncomfortable and it made him sick. Was it guilt?

Nah, fuck that, He thought to himself. *He fucked my girl Amy, and now I'm gonna fuck his.*

After Terry got up and left, he closed his eyes and took a deep breath. When he opened them the sick feeling was gone and in its place was a creepy smirk.

What you won't do for your woman another man will.

~~~~

The rest of the day passed without any major events for Brandon. There had been a few minor incidents involving small time hustlas, but besides that, nothing of importance. Unfortunately, with no real work to do, he was constantly thinking of Terry and the size of her round ass as she walked out of the café.

"Sup, mate?" O'Malley's voice thundered as he entered Brandon's office. "We're kinda done for today."

"Oh, is it already seven?" Brandon asked, checking his watch to make sure he was right. Oddly enough, he was. It seemed that the day passed quickly, after all.

Chris raised his eyebrow.

"You were a little off all day. Something wrong?"

"I'm fine, damn," Brandon grunted. "You're worse than my mother."

Chris laughed, a hearty peal that filled the room. With a wave of his hand, he left, probably eager to go home and get some rest. Brandon was eager too, but for an entirely different reason.

He looked at his phone and smiled when he saw the text from Terry. He licked his lips in expectation. It was going to be a good night.

~~~~

"I'm kind of starting to regret this," Terry said, fidgeting on the edge of the bed. "You're not going to tell him, right?"

Brandon laughed. *She's just another fucking whore. She doesn't care that she's about to screw her boyfriends brother. She only cares whether or not it will get back to him.*

"You're not serious, are you?" he uttered softly as he caressed her cheek. "I don't really root for my brother either, you know. Besides, he doesn't deserve you. You ought to have so much more," he said, laying it on thick, soothing her neglected soul.

His answer seemed to have satisfied her, because as soon as the last word left his lips, she got up and pressed her mouth against his. In a matter of seconds, the kiss turned hot. Passion was burning inside of them as they tasted each other again and again. Each stroke of the tongue hungrier than the last.

Terry was the one who broke the kiss, panting for air, a slight smirk on her wet lips.

"I haven't been kissed like this in ages," she spoke, closing in for more. When he backed away, she pouted. He pushed her back on the bed and she started giggling, her hands wrapping around his neck.

Brandon, weirdly enough, wasn't even thinking about how this would make his brother feel. He was genuinely enjoying Terry's company. He was also enjoying her lips and curvy body. Eager to please, he bent over her and their lips met again with no less desire than before. He kissed her lips, her chin and then her neck, dragging his tongue slightly across her shoulder before biting her.

She squealed softly, digging her fingernails into his back.

"You're going to leave a mark."

"I couldn't care less," he groaned against her skin, the warmth of his breath melting her.

In one swift motion, he pulled down the zipper that was in the front of her dress and quickly removed it. He was happy to see that her bra could be undone from the front as well and his eyes darkened as he exposed her full breast. He then threw the bra on the floor to join her dress.

With a satisfied smile he towered over her, admiring the roundness of her breasts. He only needed a brief moment for that. In the next one, he was kissing one, his tongue stroking the sensitive bud as his hand continued to knead the other.

"Mmm," she murmured, arching her back against the bed to give him better access. He took his time, tasting and kissing every inch of her skin as his free hand wandered down to her panties. He rubbed her pussy through the thin fabric and she lifted her hips with need.

Terry was already deliciously wet for him as she rubbed herself against his strong hand. Before she could do anything else, he slipped his fingers beneath the silk. The deliberate stroking and teasing of her swollen clit prompted loud moans from her.

Biting his lip, he eased a finger inside her. Then another. In slow motion, he pulled them in and pushed them back inside, increasing the pace as he went.

With her eyes closed, her hips followed the movement of his hand, her legs wide for his access. Little by little, she felt the orgasm building inside her. It was so close. So very close…

A frustrated groan escaped her throat when he pulled out his fingers.

"Taste yourself," he whispered, bringing his fingers to her lips. Eagerly, she grabbed his hand and licked the juices off his fingers, staring into his eyes as she did as she was told.

"What a slut," he chuckled, giving her pussy yet another rub. "Can't believe you've gone unsatisfied for so long."

With a sudden jerk, he ripped off her panties and tossed them aside. She wasn't gonna be needing those anymore. He backed up and removed his own clothes. Once he joined her on the bed, he let his shaft slide teasingly against her opening. Back and forth, he used the head of his dick to tease her soft lips.

"I hate you so much right now," she hissed, her legs spreading as wide as they could to welcome him.

He took the invitation.

With absolutely no sign of gentleness, he pushed his entire length between her silky folds, prompting a disgruntled squeal from her. He looked down at her, and much to his satisfaction, she was smirking. That was all the signal he needed to continue.

With increasing hunger, he slid his cock in and out, enjoying Terrys' loud moans. He felt her fingernails digging painfully into his back and neck, her hips quickly adjusting to his pace. Sensing her pleasure, he began to move even faster, ramming his dick mercilessly into her. Her desperate moans of pleasure invaded his ears and mind, making him crazy with lust.

"Fuck, you feel so good," he growled in her ear, biting her earlobe as he kept pounding her.

Her fingers tightened on the back of his neck, her eyes fixing him with a beast-like gaze. It was clear to him that she loved the way he was delivering the dick more than anything. He almost felt bad for her. It must've been torture for such a hungry little slut to remain untouched. *My brother's a damn fool.*

"I'm so close," she breathed out, her legs wrapping tightly around his waist. "Fill me up, Brandon. Give me all of it!"

As you wish, he thought. With renewed determination, Brandon reached down and lifted her legs over his shoulders. He shoved his dick deep into her tunnel, pushing even further once he hit bottom.

Terry's eyes rolled in the back of her head as her orgasm was finally released. Like a flood gate it washed through her, tearing carnal cries from her lips as she held on for dear life. Nothing in her life had prepared her for the sensation taking over her body.

Brandon's onslaught continued as he worked to claim his own release. Once he heard Terry cry out, he knew his own nut was soon to come. With his dick slamming hard against her folds, he gripped her tighter while burying his face against the side of her neck. Again and again he pounded into her, until with one last powerful thrust, his body tensed with fulfillment.

Spasm after spasm, had him clutching her hips making sure she couldn't move. He filled her with his juice while she continued to scream out his name in his ear. He refused to let go until he unloaded it all into her.

Panting, he collapsed on top of her, kissing her sweaty neck.

"That was amazing," he heard her murmur, her face buried into his shoulder. "Let's do it again."

"We will," he spoke as he rolled off her and took her into his arms. "We definitely will."

CHAPTER 12

Terry looked stunning that evening as she stood in front of the mirror, putting her makeup on. Malik couldn't help but wonder what he did to deserve such a beautiful woman in his life.

"What's the occasion?" he asked, gently removing her hair from her neck, leaning in to kiss it. She froze, her lips thinning into a disapproving expression.

"You're going to make my perfume wear off," she said calmly, pushing him away. She checked the mirror to reposition her hair. "And I'm just going out with my girls."

He raised his eyebrows.

"Really now? You've been spending most of your evening's with those girls for months now."

"What are you implying?" she asked, not bothering to turn to him, her voice still calm.

"Nothing, I'm just saying."

"I have to do something while you're away, Malik. I be bored in the house alone."

"I understand," he smiled bitterly, knowing she was right. It wasn't right of him to leave her alone all the time. He just had so much shit to handle and it didn't leave much time to take her out like he wanted. "Well, have fun. I'll be home by morning."

"Where are you going?"

"Someone's gotta bring in the cash," he replied as he walked out of their room.

He didn't like the fact that she was spending so much time with her slutty ass friends. He had met them and he was sure as hell they weren't right for her. They were exactly the type of bitches he hated in school – living off of their parents' money, thinking they were better than everyone else and switching men like panties.

Unfortunately, he hadn't noticed the coldness she always displayed when he tried touching her. The annoyed looks she cast him whenever he talked. Even worse, he didn't notice the marks her new lover left on her body. They were well hidden under her clothes, but that was nothing but proof of how often he touched her.

Malik got into his Mercedes and drove away. *Let her go out for as long as she wanted*, he thought. He had more important things to worry about. Such as finding out who the fuck was messing with his business.

For almost a year, they had been breaking into his houses and killing his men like they were pigs sent to slaughter. Shit was getting serious. Almost no one wanted to work with him anymore, for fear of being brutally murdered.

He stopped at the red light, yawning. A 2Pac song came up on the radio and he turned up the volume. As he listened to the lyrics he made an oath to himself. He was going to catch whoever dared to mess with his shit and personally break off his fucking neck.

Malik was so busy focusing on what he would do once he caught the men responsible for his drop in business, that he didn't notice Terry powdering her nose in the taxi right next to him. As soon as the light turned green, they separated again, both heading to handle some business.

~~~~

They were alone in the hotel room. The same hotel room their affair began in and the same one they continued it in. The same room Brandon used to fuck Terry senseless, all the while forcing useful information out of her. The same room he made untrue promises of loyalty and affection as he plotted and made moves to tear down his brothers empire.

Although the bits and pieces of information she fed him helped, she was beginning to lose her usefulness. She has been up under him so often with her legs spread that she wasn't home enough to hear any details from Malik about his business.

That was when he decided that he didn't need her anymore. Not for information, at least. In fact, he came to realize that outside of fucking, she was just in the way. Basically, she was starting to piss him off.

Like tonight. He was supposed to be watching a house in the city that he suspected was where Malik had moved his headquarters. Instead, he was stuck in the hotel with her. He didn't even know why he accepted her invitation. *Of course you do. It was your dick that made the decision.*

"Tonight's get together was kind of unplanned, don't you think?" he asked, circling the glass of wine he held as he fixed her with a hard look.

"Well, I didn't know how to tell you," she smiled, fidgeting in her chair. "And I wanted it to be to your face instead of over the phone." It was plain to see that she was making a conscious effort to look comfortable.

"Tell me what?" he asked, already expecting the worst.

"I'm pregnant."

Silence.

The words still echoed in his ears, the voice getting sharper each time it played in his mind. Louder and sharper until he couldn't take it anymore and he crushed the glass in his hand. The shards pierced his skin and small drops of blood mixed with the wine as it fell on the clean table cloth.

"What did you say?"

She didn't seem too bothered by his reaction. On the contrary, she looked rather happy. Did she even notice the glass shattering in his hand?

"I said I'm pregnant," she repeated, the smile on her face growing wider. "Aren't you happy? You're gonna be a daddy!"

It sounded so stupid. Brandon Baker, father of a child that was created while fucking his brother's woman. It was so stupid in fact that the only reaction he had was to burst into laughter. He threw his head back and let out a loud peal. A maniacal sound that seemed more of a howl than a laugh. And it frightened her.

"How do you even know it's mine?" he asked, wiping a tear from the corner of his eye.

"You're the only one I've had sex with these past months," she said, simply. "Malik has been too busy with his work. You already know this Brandon."

"You told me you were on the pill," Brandon accused, angrily.

"I know, but I stopped taking them," she said softly. "I thought..."

"You fuckin' bitch," he snapped, cutting her off. "You really thought it would've been a good idea? Ya really thought I would've been happy about this, huh?"

"I just—"

"I just… I just…" he mocked her. "You just what? You thought I wanted a kid with you? After a few months of fucking? Dumb ass whore," he said, shaking his head in disgust.

Terry was shaking. The happiness she felt just a few minutes ago turned into despair, and the despair into anger. Her fist violently met the table, the glass shards clinking softly at the impact.

"You fucking bastard!" she yelled. "You fucking low life coward!"

She reached for the wine bottle and aimed it at his head, but he was faster. He grabbed her wrist, his fingers digging painfully into her flesh as he took the bottle and threw it away.

"I hate you!" she shouted, and spit in his face.

He felt the liquid dripping from his face. With a calm motion, he took a napkin and wiped it off as if it had been nothing. He then yanked her close to him and shoved it into her mouth.

"Get the fuck out of my room," he hissed through his teeth, forcing her back. He then pulled her towards the door and threw her out as if she had only been a rag.

All the air left her lungs in a painful whoosh as she hit the wall behind her in the hallway. The heel of her shoe broke and she fell to the floor. She covered her face and began to sob uncontrollably.

Brandon was standing in the doorway, staring at her with an amused look on his face.

"Can't wait to see how you deal with this shit," he laughed, examining the cuts on his hand. "I imagine my bro won't be so happy about this."

Terry didn't say anything.

"Can you imagine?" he continued. He loved twisting the knife in the wound. "He saw you as some fuckin' goddess fallen from the Heavens to earth. And what are you? Just a dirty whore who cheated on him with his own brother. And guess what? You'll be the only one held accountable for it."

And, with one last chuckle, he went back inside his room, locking the door behind him. After seeing to his hand, he made sure everything was in order before he left. When he opened the door to leave, she was nowhere to be found.

~~~~

Terry looked at her reflection in the mirror. Her eyes were bloodshot and swollen, black lines of eyeliner were smeared on her cheeks. Her hair was a fucking mess. It was sticking up in every direction and making her look like a crazy woman.

She stared into her reflection's eyes and saw... nothing. She was numb. She couldn't feel anything anymore. It was like she had been sedated. No, that was not the right word. Zombie worked better for her situation. She was a zombie. A shadow of the woman she was just a few hours ago.

Taking a deep breath, she washed her face, cleaning every trace of makeup off her skin before applying a fresh layer. She had to look as if nothing happened when she got back home. She couldn't let Malik suspect anything.

She'd made up her mind about her situation. She was going to tell Malik that she was pregnant with *his* child and hope he would be too excited to realize that it was technically impossible. Especially since they hadn't had sex in months except for that one night a couple of months ago when he came home half drunk. Although the whole ordeal was over before it started, she hoped it would be enough to convince him.

Luckily for her, there was no one home when she arrived. Now she could take a few more minutes to gather together her thoughts. An hour had passed by when she finally heard the door open. Instantly her heart started racing.

"Babe?" she heard Maliks' voice from downstairs. "You home?"

She ran down the stairs and threw herself in his arms. He hugged her back, a mix of surprise and worry on his face.

"Baby, what happened? What's wrong?" he asked, alarmed.

She looked up at him, cupping his face and planting a soft kiss on his lips before telling him.

"You're gonna be a father."

His eyes widened, but his expression was totally different from his brother's when the same words were spoken to him. He looked genuinely happy and she breathed out in relief. *He bought it.*

"Are you serious?" he asked, a big grin on his handsome face. "How... When did you... Oh, god, this is so great!"

"This morning. I felt kinda bad, so I suspected something like this. Well, I went to buy a pregnancy test and it came out positive! Aren't you excited?"

"I am!" he exclaimed, kissing her over and over again. He gently rubbed her belly, looking at her with tears in his eyes. "I'm gonna be a daddy! Me! Ma's gonna go crazy when I tell her. We should throw a party and invite her and my bro too."

"No!" she shrieked. "I mean," she coughed, fixing her voice. "You really think that would be a good idea? Your brother is a cop, after all. I don't trust him enough to be around your buddies without causing trouble."

Malik nodded, agreeing with her. It might make his boys nervous.

"You're right. I'll just invite my mom then, how's that?"

"Better," she smiled. "Much better."

CHAPTER 13

The party had been going for a few hours and was now in full swing. He let his eyes roam around the house, taking note of a few close friends and some relatives the family stayed in contact with. He didn't want to throw the party in his house, seeing as it was riddled with guns and drugs, so he chose his mother's house instead. Despite everything she knew about his friends, Gloria found them to be good people and she always enjoyed their company.

Everything would have been perfect if Brandon would have been there. Unfortunately, he had called at the last minute saying he had to work and couldn't get out of it. Malik didn't know if it was true or not, but he couldn't find fault in him not being there. *A man's gotta work, right?*

Just then, Malik turned and smiled over at his mother. She was hovering over Terry making sure she didn't want or need anything. She had been so ecstatic when they told her they were having a baby. This would be her first grandchild and she couldn't wait to jump into her role of being a Grandma.

Terry glanced over at Malik and they shared a private moment of fulfillment when their eyes met. She knew that Malik loved her and she loved him as well. If she could convince him to leave the *game* sooner than later and move to another area, she could try to avoid running into Brandon. It would lower the risk of him ever telling Malik about their affair and that he was the father of her child. She would do whatever it takes to protect her baby and her relationship with Malik. *I won't fuck up again.*

Malik made a funny face at Terry and she laughed. He was about to make his way over to her when his cell phone vibrated in his pocket. He gave Terry a wink and then went into the only room in the house that nobody was allowed in – his old bedroom. By the time Malik locked the door, the phone stopped vibrating. He stared down at the glowing screen, the odd sequence of numbers unfamiliar to him. The phone began vibrating again, and he took a moment before answering.

"Yeah," he called out cautiously. He knew his phone couldn't be getting tapped because he never kept them long enough for the police to get a lock on it.

From the other side, a familiar voice greeted him. He could feel his heartbeats slowing down, knowing it was someone he knew. But why was he calling from another number?

"M—M—Malik, my f—friend," Drake's stammering voice called out to him. If he didn't know better, he would've thought he was scared. Instead, his little speech impairment made him grin as always. "I h—have some imp—p—ortant stuff to t—tell you, man."

"What you got for me Drake?" he asked, making the man get to the point.

"I found out who's b—b—been fuckin' wi—with your business, man."

"Go on," Malik hissed through his teeth. He had waited for this moment for so long. Gruesome images unveiled themselves before his eyes, each depicting a painful way he would deal with the man who had been fucking with his empire.

"It's b—been the p—police all this time m—man!" the other man stuttered, a slight note of nervousness in his voice. "L—look man, I really have t—t—to go, but I have ev—everything you n—n—need to know. You know w—where to find me."

And without another word, he ended the call.

Malik began to smile. He had been waiting for this particular piece of information for almost a year now and finally hearing it, made him happy. Although he would need more details and information, he was happy knowing he'd finally caught a break.

After pushing the phone back in his pocket, Malik dug in his other pocket and pulled out a plastic package. It was small, but filled to the bursting point with white powder. It was more than a few grams of coke and It would be his token of appreciation to Drake.

The man had been working for him for the past few years and had never let him down. He was a cocaine addict, among other things, but he has been loyal to him from day one. Malik had been lucky to catch Drake when he just started as a rookie. Unfortunately, he was a cop with a habit. After a few free grams of coke, he had accepted the agreement from Malik to offer information regarding the police and other dealers, in return for a nice fix.

Humming *O.T. Genasis, I'm In Love With The Coco*, he left the room. Making sure no one saw him, he left out of the house through the back door. The party was important, sure. But so was his business. He had to go talk to Drake and he had to do it right now before he got high and disappeared.

~~~~

Drake woke up to the sound of several loud bangs on his door. *God fuckin' damn it! The doorbell button was there for a fuckin' reason.*

He got up and scratched his ass, wondering who the fuck was bothering him at that hour of the night. If it was that bum from the corner store again asking for money he'd put a bullet in his dumbass head.

With rising anger, he peered through the keyhole and saw a rather huge man standing in front of his door. He was about to pussy out and step away quietly when he heard the voice on the other side.

"Nigga, you gonna open the door or what?"

Shit. Shit, shit, shit! What was Malik doing there at that hour? Sure, he called him to give him the info, but he wasn't actually expecting the man to show up like that in the middle of the fuckin' night.

"Yeah, man," he said as he opened the door and Malik stepped in, larger than life. Drake felt a chill ease down his spine. This was one mother fucker he didn't ever want to go up against. Gun or no gun.

"Wassup with you coming by at this hour, man? I was having a really nice dream."

"What happened to the stutter?" Malik asked, raising his eyebrow. His voice was like steel.

Drake coughed and then smiled. "Yeah, that shit is just for show. I always make my calls to you from a public booth," he shrugged. "I made a habit out of doing that shit outside just in case I was being watched or followed."

"Phone booth?" *This punk little fucker better not be trying to set me up.* Malik looked around the small living room, making sure they were alone.

"Yeah, it's like the only one left around here. Its by the movie theatre so they keep it for emergencies." When he saw Malik looking around, he swallowed hard knowing he had to reassure him. "We're alone."

Malik looked down at Drake and frowned. "So you don't stutter? What other shit you been lying about?" he asked as he walked over and opened a door that was closed, checking inside.

"Nothing Malik. I swear. And it wasn't lying. I was just making sure to cover my tracks you know. I'm a cop man and I need to keep my job. It's the only way I can pay for my son's daycare expenses."

After Malik was satisfied they were alone, he walked back over to Drake.

"Don't make me nervous Drake. That's how people get hurt or end up missing. You feel me?"

Drake nodded. "Yeah, I got it. It's all for my protection, man," he said, a shadow of a grin crossing his face. "You never know who might be following you. And with the shit I know, I wouldn't be surprised if there was someone at my door right now," he said, gesturing for Malik to take a seat in the small living room.

Malik took a seat in one of the high backed chairs across from Drake. He could feel the steel of his Nine pressing into his stomach, but he took the pain. He needed to be on point. *Just in case.*

"You told me the police is behind all this shit," he began. "But can you tell me who exactly is leading the operations? I fuckin' paid every boss that works there so they'd keep their dirty fuckin' noses outta my shit."

Drake shook his head.

"Nah, man. I'm not trusted enough in there just yet to know that kinda shit, but I do know that the guy is not new. Just think about it. A rookie wouldn't have even dared to do such shit. Too scared for that, ya dig?"

"Makes sense," Malik nodded. "Does anyone else know, though?"

"Nah. I heard that it's some hard nose cop that got a promotion after making a shit load of arrest. They say the boss put him in charge of a special unit. The guy now has a team of go getters, but they don't say nothing about them or the guy himself. They keep their shit secret for fear of leaks and what not," he laughed at his irony. It was a pathetic bellow that turned into an ugly coughing fit. "Anyway," he continued after the coughing stopped, "I heard some people saying that there is no actual boss or team, and its regular police officers that's running down on you, but I know a bit of the truth."

"And what's that?" Malik asked, leaning forward.

"I know for sure that there is a guy that leads the special unit and the team members are forbidden by contract to talk about him. I tried questioning some of the detectives, but none of them would talk to me."

"So basically," Malik sighed, "what you told me is pretty much useless."

Drake smirked. It was the smirk of a man who knew more than he showed.

"The thing is," he continued. "I was speaking to the wrong fuckin' people, man. I just needed to find a weak link. There's a guy at the precinct that is maybe jealous of this team leader guy or angry at the jobs he's given. I don't know. What I do know is that the smallest things upsets him. And he's a bit of a drinker."

Malik's eyes widened. If the previous minute marked the moment he'd lost hope, this one brought it back doubled. He looked at the man in front of him. A twenty-something police officer with a cocaine addiction. It wasn't known to no one but him, and he had promised to keep his secret. It was a shame too, because Drake was incredibly intelligent. He just couldn't beat his habit. *But could he be trusted?*

For a brief second, he felt a pang of fear creeping into his heart. How could he be so sure that Drake wouldn't turn against him and team up with the so-called good guys? He reached down into his pocket and felt the small bag of coke he hid there. That was the exact reason Drake Moore would stay loyal to him. He needed his fix and Malik had the best shit out on the streets.

"So, as I was saying," Drake uttered, licking his lips in anticipation. "I found the weak link, man. I don't know his name or anything like that because he refused to tell it, but he accepted to tell me about his boss' plans and shit. It cost me 2 bottles of top shelf Vodka and $200 bucks that I hope to be refunded."

Malik nodded. "No problem." He dug in his pocket and quickly pulled off five hundred dollars and tossed it on the glass table between them.

"That's what's up," Drake said nodding. "Aight, so this is what's going down. Get your downtown house ready on Tuesday. They're gonna raid it at around seven that night. I think it would be wise to just clear the whole place out a few days before. Ya don't wanna risk anything."

"Maybe," Malik said, thinking to himself. While he tossed a few thoughts around in his head, he reached in his pocket and pulled out the plastic bag full of coke. "I got a few more questions for ya, and while ya answer them, I got ya something sweet," he said tossing the bag next to the money.

As the white bag landed on the table, Drake's eyes widened in something that could only be described as feral hunger. He snatched the bag up and opened it, digging his nose deeply into the powder. Taking a quick sniff, he sat back, sighing in pleasure.

"I swear don't nobody got shit like yours, man." Needing another hit, Drake took his wallet from his back pocket and slid out his bank card. He poured a bit of white powder on the glass table and separated it neatly in four thin rows with the credit card. He then picked up one of the hundred dollar bills Malik had just given him and cleared away one of the lines. "Ask away," he said already feeling the drug racing through him.

"This guy ya told me about, the snitch, was he involved in the past raids?"

He had to wait for Drake to snort another line of cocaine through the rolled up bill that was now a tube, before getting his answer.

"Yeah, I think so. Why? You think there's more than one team?"

"Kinda, yeah. It's seems impossible for only one to do all this shit. They hitting my houses all over the place. Not just in one area."

"Nah, man," Drake said, carefully closing the bag and putting it in his wallet. "It's only one team of motherfuckers."

"And why did this guy step out just now? I don't know, man, it just seems kinda shady to me, that's all."

"He's cool. All he cared about was the money and keeping his glass filled. The thing is, he started really hating on the man. He said his success got to his head and shit."

"And you sure you can't get me there names? Not even through the computer?" Malik asked. He noticed how glassy Drakes eyes had gotten and knew he would soon be useless.

"Nah, man, can't do it. The whole place would get shut down and we'd all get interrogated. They would know that if their names came out, it was internal."

Malik nodded.

"I still want you to try again. Work on that guy some more. Buy his ass as many bottles as he wants. I got you."

"I'll try," Drake said and shrugged. "But don't count on that. He might have wised up. I'd be more focused on getting your places ready for the raids if I were you, to be honest."

"Don't worry about that," Malik smiled cruelly. "When those fuckers get there they'll have the surprise of their fucking lives."

"Man, I wish I could see the looks on their faces," Drake laughed. He could only imagine the whole crew, armed and furious, ready to cause some serious havoc, only to find themselves standing in the middle of an empty house. Too bad he couldn't be there to see it.

~~~~

As Malik watched over the empty house from his hiding spot, a feeling of excitement washed over him. It had been a while since he felt what he could only compare to as the joy a kid gets on Christmas day. He was dying to finally catch the motherfuckers responsible. He was constantly taking a loss financially and he was tired of it.

Finally, a black SUV with tinted windows pulled over. For a few minutes, nothing happened. Malik assumed they were only getting their strategy clear once more. They didn't have to worry about that, though – they would have nothing to take over.

With a loud thud, the door opened and the first pair of combat boots slammed on the pavement. A wave of discontent rushed over Malik as he saw that the man's face was covered by a black ski mask. What the fuck were these assholes planning to do with his people? Gas them?

He only counted three men by the time the string of his thoughts was broken by the sudden vibrations of his phone.

He ignored it.

It stopped and then started again, worrying him. People usually don't call twice unless it's something urgent. By the time he fished it out of his pocket, it stopped once again. As he unlocked it, another short vibration announced a text message. It was from Flea, one of his men.

Man Down @24. u gotta hurry.

Fuck this shit! 24th was a house he owned in the centre and he remembered making the mistake of not having enough people to guard it. And now, his mistake cost him the life of one of his men. The police gang could wait. He had more important shit to do at the moment.

~~~~

Brandon got out of the car just as Malik left. He fixed his shirt's cuffs and took another look at his perfectly polished boots as if he was preparing for an important meeting. You could say that, actually. It would be just another step in bringing his brother down.

"A'ight," he spat at his crew. "We know they're here and we know exactly how many they are. Let's do this!"

As usual, he didn't need encouragement speeches or motivational words. They had all the damn motivation they needed – putting bullets through those bastards' filthy skulls.

They crept through the dark street to the doorway in silence, knowing that the slightest noise could give them away. Brandon could feel his pulse racing. It was like a drug to him now. The terror those men felt when they were faced with the last seconds of their life gave him an unseen rush. He experienced a liberating feeling when he pulled the trigger and he felt a tingle of ecstasy that ran through his veins when he saw them lying in pools of their own blood. *It was better than sex*, he thought insanely.

"At my command," he whispered when they were finally at the door.

He waited for a few more seconds, allowing his men the moment they needed to get ready and when they all looked set, he shouted, "Now!"

He kicked the door open, the fragile wood breaking under the force of his foot.

"Drop your guns, motherfuckers!" he yelled, running into the main hall. "Did you hear me? Drop your gu— "

"Boss," Chris said, approaching him from the back of the house. He looked oddly relaxed, given the conditions. Brandon looked around and much to his dismay, the rest of his men had their guns down. "There's no one here. We've looked around and this shit hole is empty."

"What the hell do you mean empty?" he asked confused.

"He means it's fuckin' empty," Trev spat, walking out of the living room. "You got the wrong Intel, chief."

Brandon looked around at his team. The confused look on his face soon turned into irritation at his crew's amused expressions. They were right. The house was empty and he could tell they were thinking he was the one to blame for the lost time and wasted effort.

"Let's get outta here," he growled, walking out.

FALSE

He could feel their mocking looks burning through the back of his skull.

CHAPTER 14

"So how was your week?" Sergeant Hardy asked, leaning back away from his desk. He was smiling, but it was more of a sneer. He wasn't proud of Brandon's last couple of assignments coming up empty. The Mayor wanted answers and he could only get them from Brandon. "Heard your radar is kinda messed up lately."

Brandon took a deep breath. He had to muster a lot of patience to deal with his Sergeant, especially since he was right about his fuckups.

"I received the wrong info from my source, that's all. I think we might've been misguided on purpose."

Sergeant Hardy snorted, making Brandon's blood boil. He reminded him of Malik looking down at him with a scornful expression. Whenever he did something that didn't rise up to his standards he would give him that look. He then would see his mother, shaking her head and looking at him in disapproval. He felt a lump of resentment in his throat and struggled to swallow it.

"We can't keep doing this shit anymore, Baker," Hardy said, choosing a cigarette from his pack. "Would you fetch me the lighter?"

He did as he was told, handing the silver lighter to his boss. The man lit the cigarette and took a long drag, watching the smoke rise to the ceiling. It filled the room with a bitter smell. Brandon could barely hold in a cough.

"These thugs and gangsta's are starting to take you guys for fools. You're supposed to be feared and obeyed around here, but lately it seems like they're playing you. And I don't like that at all, Baker. Most importantly, the Mayor doesn't like it."

"Sir, that's not my fault. I just— "

"It is your fault!" he yelled, slamming his hand down hard against his desk. Hardy drew in another puff of smoke and pushed it out through his nose. He narrowed his eyes and pinned him down with his stare. "It's your informant, your source, so it's your fucking fault! Furthermore, I don't care whose fault it is. You're in charge, so deal with it. You got that!?"

God, how I want to punch his fuckin' ugly nose in. How dare he treat me like that? Who the fuck did this asshole think he was?

"Yeah, I got it," Brandon hissed through gritted teeth. It took all the strength he could muster to utter those words.

"Good. Now get outta my office!"

He opened his mouth to say something, but decided to leave well enough alone. It was incredible how the man whom he had respected the most just became the one person he hated just as much as his brother. And it only took a couple of minutes of him screaming at him knowing damn well, everyone on the floor could hear him. Of course, his anger was justified, but that didn't mean he had to treat him like a piece of shit.

Closing the door behind him, Brandon shuttered with annoyance. This shit looked bad and he was fucking embarrassed by the side looks he was getting. He needed to fix this shit, no matter the cost. Then he would take care of that piece of shit that humiliated him just a few moments ago.

The loud voices of his colleagues turned into murmurs as soon as he passed through the precinct. He knew he was the cause and did everything he could to ignore them. The two secretaries who had been busy gossiping until then pointed at him and started to giggle. *It was no different from a high school in this place*, he thought as he kept it moving. You could be the top dog to everyone one minute, but as soon as you took a wrong step, you became the main joke.

People really didn't grow up at all, no matter how much they denied it. They were teens trapped in adult bodies, ready to mock and belittle anyone who dared to make a mistake. It didn't matter, though. He'll show them. He'll show them once and for all that Brandon Baker was not a man to be messed with.

~~~~

Malik was sitting on the porch with a large bottle of Rémy Martin next to him. It had been a calm few days, and business was going steady. The money had started rolling in as it used to. On top of that, thanks to Moore, his men weren't afraid of the police showing up at their doorsteps and killing them anymore. He had been delivering information on the norm and it was on point. No more run downs on his trap houses.

He looked at his girlfriend, sunbathing in the yard, her little round belly shining from all the sunscreen she applied on it. A sudden wave of happiness washed over him that had his heart racing like crazy. What was that odd feeling? Was it love? Probably. He loved his woman, of course, and he loved his unborn child.

He thought about all the things he would do for him. He would send him to a good school and make sure he wouldn't have to miss his childhood years like he did. Maybe he would become a doctor or a teacher or even a cop, like his uncle Brandon.

A slight chuckle escaped his lips as he thought of that. Brandon would make a great teacher for his nephew. A much better one than his own father, the drug dealer. Could he ever tell him? *Maybe*, he thought. *When he's old enough to understand.*

But what if you won't be there to explain, the annoying voice of his conscience echoed in his head.

He hated how right it was and he wished he had the power to ignore it. But the truth was, he couldn't. Ever since he found out he was going to be a father, the same thought ate him up from the inside. What would happen if he got murdered or died suddenly in an accident like his father? His son would have to grow up without his dad, seeing his mom withering away as the days passed.

Fuck that! He wouldn't let that happen. He loved life and he planned to enjoy it until he died of old age. And in case something happened, he would make sure to leave Terry enough money to care for their son without having to struggle like his own mother did.

And hopefully, his son wouldn't grow up to be like him. Hopefully.

~~~~

Drake's blood froze in his veins when he heard the door opening. There was no way he could hide in time and if he did, the scattered papers on Brandon's desk would still arise suspicion.

Shit, that was bad. That was very, very bad. Only a miracle could save him and miracles never happened to people like him.

"What the fuck are you doing in here?" Brandon growled, locking the door behind him after he stepped in, much to Drake's horror.

He cleared his throat, not wanting to sound insecure. That was the last thing he needed.

"Chief sent me in here to fetch him some papers. I just got back from his office and I thought— ”

“You thought you'd come in my office without asking for permission and go through my shit.”

“He told me to hurry and I didn't know where you were.”

Brandon grinned, a wolfish smirk that stood Drake's hair on its ends.

“I'll have you know,” he said, slowly approaching the man. “That I was just in the chief's office until now and I didn't see you in there.”

“I—I just— ”

“What were you doing with my papers?”

“Nothing, I just— ”

“I'll ask you again,” he growled. “What. Were you doing. WITH MY FUCKIN' PAPERS?”

Without waiting for an answer, he hurried over to the desk, grabbing the file from Drake's shaking hands. When he opened it, he felt his pulse slowing. As he went through the pages, he saw the marked locations on the maps. The fucker was trying to steal the maps. But why?

Suddenly, something clicked in his head. He was a rookie transfer, hired not long ago. In fact, he happened to show up just when the houses he tried to raid had been found empty. That shit was no coincidence.

“So it was you,” he laughed. A maniacal peal that rose to the gray ceiling, making Drake cower in fear. “It was you all along. You're the snitch.” A chuckle slid through his lips as he grabbed the man's shirt, forcing him to look up at him. “Do you know what you did?”

Drake shook his head.

“You don't know?” Brandon thundered, droplets of spit hitting Moore's face.

“No! No, I don't know!” he cried out, desperate to escape. Brandon's grip on him was too tight, though.

“You made a fool outta me. You made a fuckin' fool outta me and now you gotta pay up.”

“No, please,” he begged. “I'll leave. I'll do anything you want. Just let me go.”

“Let you go?” Brandon smirked. “Oh, no, no. I got better plans for you, bitch.”

~~~~

The house was empty, as Brandon had expected it to be. It seemed that the motherfuckers didn't even bother coming back and cleaning the mess. The door was still broken from the last time he'd been there.

He went back outside and paused for a second in the doorway, thinking about a faster way he could get Moore inside. He was passed out in the back of his car, an ugly dark bruise already forming on his temple from where he was hit with his gun's handle. He didn't really give Brandon a choice. He kept whining and bitching for almost half an hour before he had tried to throw himself out of the car.

He dragged him out of the car and into the house, his jeans ripping as they slid against the pavement. He took him downstairs, in the basement that had been previously used as a meeting place for the thugs.

He thought dragging Drake into the basement was hard, but changed his mind the second he had to lift him up to place him on the chair. Finally, after a few minutes of struggling, he managed to get the man on the chair.

Wiping the sweat off his forehead, he took the rope from around his waist and started the second part of the job. His hands were first, safely bound to one another behind his back, while his legs were tied to the chair. When he made sure the knots wouldn't snap, he used the rest of the rope to secure his waist to the wooden chair.

He took a few moments to admire his work, cracking a slight smile at the sight of the passed out man.

"Wake up, Sleeping Beauty," he uttered as he slapped the man hard as hell.

Drake's eyes cracked open, still narrowed as they adjusted to the dim light. It seemed that he didn't know where he was, so Brandon decided to remind him. When the back of his hand met the man's face, he yelped in pain, his eyes widening at the sight of the almost empty room.

"Where the fuck am I?" he cried. "Let me go!"

"You're not in the position to give orders right now, you know? So if I were you, I'd be keeping my mouth shut, motherfucker!"

Drake groaned, his hand moving frantically behind his back as he tried to escape the rope's painful hold. But it was so tightly bound that he ended up hurting himself even more.

"It'll be over before you realize it started," Brandon laughed, reaching for the knife he had on his belt. He carefully placed it on the table behind Drake, along with his gun, his badge and his tazer. He checked his pockets and belt for anything he might've forgotten. He decided he was only going to use one thing – the knife.

"What are you doing with that?" Drake asked, his voice shaking in terror.

Brandon didn't answer. Instead, he caressed the blade of his knife, tracing the edge with his finger. Small droplets of blood stained the steel – it was perfect.

"Who did you sell the info to?" he asked calmly.

"No one. It's just a misunderstanding!"

A painful blow landed on his right cheek. The man groaned, spitting some blood on the floor. Not a pretty sight.

"I'll ask again," Brandon smiled, dragging the blade to the man's shoulder. He shivered when the cold steel touched his skin. A gasp escaped his lips when he felt it rising up to the base of his neck. "And if you don't give me a satisfying answer, this lil' boy here will have you sleeping with the fishes in no time. I'll just toss your body in the lake and no one will ever know who did it."

Drake closed his eyes, struggling to swallow the painful lump at the back of his throat. He wasn't a snitch. He knew very well what the price for that was. But on the other hand, he'd very much liked to live. He was pretty sure he could escape Malik's anger and run away to start a new life somewhere else. He still had enough cocaine left to sell for good money so that wouldn't be a problem. The biggest problem was the cop. He couldn't escape him, no matter what. Unless he told him everything he knew about Malik's business.

"To their leader," he finally spoke.

"What's his name?" He knew who he was, of course. He just wanted to hear him say it.

"Malik. Malik Brown," he said, spitting out Malik's alias. No one knew his real last name.

Suddenly the man screamed. A sudden wave of pain shot through his body, starting from his shoulder. He looked at it and saw a gushing wound, freshly made by Brandon's knife.

"How much did he pay you?"

Fighting back the tears, he stammered.

"H—He didn't give me m—money. He only gave me some blow."

A guttural peal of laughter escaped Brandon's throat. He should've known he was a junkie. They were the easiest to use. Just a gram of what they were addicted to would have them on their knees obeying your every command. He had thought about using that trick many times, but it was too risky for a police officer to be caught owning drugs. It was a risk he was not willing to take.

"Blow," he chuckled. "You did it for coke? Why couldn't you do it for me? I would've given you money."

"He came to me first," Drake whined.

Another wound opened, this time on his upper arm. Brandon dragged the knife slowly through his flesh, applying just the right amount of pressure to cause enough pain with minimum damage.

"You should've known who you were fuckin' with," he said, slapping the back of his head. "Everyone knows that I'm the king of the streets now. Not my brother."

"Your what?" asked Drake, a disbelieving look on his face.

Drake couldn't believe his ears. His brother? Malik Brown, the uncontested king of the streets was Brandon's brother? *What the fuck did I just get mixed up in?*

"My brother," Brandon said laughing. Seeing the confused expression on the man's face, he felt the need to explain. "Not many people know that about us, since from what I've heard, he refuses to give out his family name. Security reasons, ya know."

"But if he's your brother, why are you fucking with his business?" Drake asked, hoping he could take Brandon's mind off torturing him.

"Fuck him," the man replied, jabbing the knife in Drake's upper thigh. He squealed like a pig, prompting a small chuckle from Brandon.

"One last question," he began. The flicker of hope in the man's eyes made him grin. "How much does he know about my operations?"

"As much as I've told him," Drake immediately replied. "Only about the first five houses."

"Good."

A loud bang echoed in the room. Drake Moore was no more.

CHAPTER 15

"So I was tellin' her – bitch, if ya ain't gonna pay, then get down on your knees and suck this dick."

The glass chandelier rattled slightly at the sudden peals of laughter. There were about five men sitting around a table filled with bottles and empty glasses. A few beer cans were lying under the table, alongside the two men who'd had a little too much alcohol. The remaining ones were discussing their latest affairs, counting their money, and laughing at the occasional jokes.

All in all, it was a pretty chill evening in one of Malik's houses on South 16th Street. The crew liked to call it, *The Pit.*

Suddenly, a loud bang at the door interrupted their laughter.

"Who the fuck is it?" one of the men asked, cocking his gun.

No answer.

They all looked at each other and then back to the exit, most of them having their guns ready.

"If ya don't answer," the same man continued, "we'll come out and pop a cap in yo ass."

Still no reply. They got tense. They knew that whenever one of their men would visit the house, he wouldn't even bother knocking. He'd just come in, toss his gun on the table and grab a beer or whatever. As for Malik, that couldn't have been him either. He had gone to Atlantic City to sort out some business.

Before they knew it, the door slammed into the wall, and five armed men stormed in. Their bullets were useless against the heavily protected intruders who didn't waste a second and started shooting each and every one of Malik's hustlas.

"Shoot on sight," Brandon had told his men as they had been waiting for his orders. "Leave no motherfucker alive, be it man or woman."

He was pleased to see that they had listened to him. After a few moments, the men were dead and the ones who had been lying under the table were executed while unconscious.

Once they made sure everything was safe, they took off their helmets and went to search the house. All except for Brandon who took a seat at the round table, grabbing all the money in front of him. A cigar was still lit and he took a puff. *Cuban*, he thought, blowing out the thick smoke. *Good shit.*

"How much?" Chris asked, nudging one of the bodies with his foot.

"About 30 grand. We'll split, as always."

Chris nodded. Despite everything, he loved working for Brandon. Not only did he get his salary at the precinct, but any money they found in the drug houses was theirs to keep. He made more cash over the last few months than he did in his whole life so far. And he was going to make damn sure that Brandon was going to keep his job as long as possible.

~~~~

Finally back home, Malik was lying in bed, an open book by his side and a glass of Rémy on his nightstand. He was about to fall asleep when his phone rang. Recognizing the name of one of his men, he didn't want to answer at first. But after seeing how it stopped ringing, it started up again, he finally picked up.

"Malik, man," Meek spoke in a grave tone. "It's bad. Really, really bad."

He knew what he meant before he even told him.

"Where?"

"The Pit. Look, man, I'm at your place right now, parked. Come down and let's go there together, a'ight?"

With a deep sigh, he got up and threw on a white tshirt and some jeans. He grabbed his piece out the drawer and tucked it beneath his belt at his back. What a fuckin' mood killer. Sometimes he wished he could just give it all up and go live down south somewhere. No one would know him. Just him, his woman and his kid, all alone and free to live any way he wanted.

He looked through the window and saw the blue BMW parked in front of his house. He grabbed his hat and headed out the door, careful not to wake Terry. Down stairs, Meek's grim face when he got in the car didn't do him much good either.

"What happened?" Malik asked as they drove off.

"They raided The Pit," he spat through his teeth. "Killed all the men there and took the cash again."

"Impossible. I had a man in the precinct. He gave me info. He would've told me!"

"Ya talkin' about Drake?" Meek asked, his eyes narrowing. "Ya actually thought that coke head nigga could be trusted?"

Malik sighed, rubbing his face. He was tired.

"I had my reasons. I know for sure he'd never betray me. Have you gone by The Pit?"

"Nah, man," he shook his head. "Had no business there and it was way too far from my usual working spot. I just found out from Trev."

"Trev, huh?" Malik snorted. "How do you know HE can be trusted?"

"Look, man, this ain't a good time to start doubting each other. You trust your man and I trust mine, ya feel me?"

Malik shrugged. Meek was right. That shit didn't really matter at the moment.

"There it is," the man said, pulling over the car in The Pit's driveway. It looked bad already. The door was wide open and his men's cars were still parked around the house. When he walked into the main hall, he stared at the blood-soaked floor, a few of his men lying there with their eyes wide open.

He knelt next to a bigger-looking guy named Cash, a wave of anger washing over him as he gently closed the dead man's eyes. He had been one of the good ones. He was only doing what he needed to make sure his wife and four sons had everything they needed. He remembered how he used to show everyone pictures of them in their school uniforms, telling them how they got the highest grades in the class, and how proud he was of them.

And now the poor kids lost their only support. He thought about how they would probably be forced to move into the projects once the last of their money was spent. Malik punched the floor, blinking away the painful thoughts.

"Man, you gotta see this," Meek called to him from the living room.

As soon as he walked into the living, he froze. In the middle of the room, tied to a chair, was Drake Moore, his inside man. His face was bloody and bruised. You could tell someone worked him over with a knife all across his shoulders, arms and legs. He was completely naked, the word SNITCH carved into the flesh of his chest.

"Ya think our men did this?"

Malik shook his head.

"Nah. We don't do this shit to our people," he sighed, grabbing one of the curtains to cover Drakes' body. "We just shoot and bury. This is the work of a fuckin' psychopath."

"What do we do with the bodies and the house? This spot is hot now," said Meek.

Brandon turned away from the man tied to the chair and headed for the door.

"Burn it!"

~~~~

The second they left The Pit, Malik ordered for all his gang leaders to gather to *The Unit*. The Unit was a warehouse he owned and used to store his merchandise and money. He didn't trust banks because they asked too many questions.

It took them all about an hour to arrive. Seeing them all around the big table, Malik couldn't help but feel bad for them. He didn't tell them why they were there and they looked worried.

"We secure down stairs?" he asked, causing everyone to quiet down.

He got nods of approval from several men.

Rock walked in and stood by Brandon, Rich and Meek. The four of them were the foundation of the business with Malik at the head.

"We good Malik," Rich replied in a deadly tone. "I brought six of my beasts along and they at the doors." Rich always looked mad at the world. His face was covered in tear drops and everyone knew what they meant. They knew to keep their distance from him.

"Why ya bring us here, anyway?" Rock asked. "I got better shit to do." Rock had a scar that started from his forehead and ended right under his left eye. It was also the reason he was blind in that eye and it had turned gray. The men called him Rock because he'd lost the eye during a fight. His opponent had hit him with a sharp rock, yet he didn't live to brag about it.

A few men muttered the same question under their breath, but not too loud to draw Malik's attention.

He decided he should get straight to the point. There was no need to waste anyone's time. "Cause in case ya haven't heard our houses are being raided by the police. The most recent was The Pit. They hit that not too long ago and they killed all the men there. They also tortured and killed my snitch too, so he wasn't involved."

"Then we gotta do something," another man shouted. He was young and thin, but that didn't stop him from making a name for himself as the Cutter. One could understand why he was called that once they saw what he could do with a simple knife. "We can't let them think they can fuck with us and get away with it!"

"I thought ya were paying the sheriff good money to keep his people away from us," Rock spoke. "Does he wanna die?"

"I think they're acting on their own. They work under the police, but they aren't really controlled by them," said Malik.

"Who are they?" Rich asked. He was ready to knock some heads.

Malik shook his head.

"I've no fuckin' idea yet. That's why I asked y'all to come. I want y'all to plant cameras all around your houses. We gotta find out who the fuck they are and deal with'em."

"A'ight," Cutter nodded. "But what's gonna stop them from running down on us again?"

Malik thought for a minute. "Keep the houses guarded inside and out, but don't make it too obvious. And for fuck's sake, do your men really need to spread out the cash like that? Count it and store it. That's it. I better not see another mother fucker posting shit on the Gram or the Book with my money around them or they're dead," he said angrily.

There were no other protests from his men and the room was quiet.

"I'll take your silence as you understanding me," he said standing up. "Cameras, guards, count and then store. Get drunk and laid afterwards. We gon' catch these motherfuckers if it's the last thing we do."

CHAPTER 16

Everyone sat in the conference room of the precinct awaiting Brandon's arrival so he could begin the meeting that he'd called.

"Anyone knows what this is about?" O'Malley openly asked while sitting on the edge of the table, twirling one of his knives from one hand to the other.

No one responded. He took that as them not knowing and simply shrugged it off and continued spinning his knife. The room was so quiet you could hear a pin drop. Everyone wore an expression as if they had a lot on their minds. Then the doors to the conference room were pushed open and Brandon walked in. All eyes were on him as he made his way to the head of the table and took his seat.

"I know you all are wondering what this meeting is about."

"What gave it away?" O'Malley smirked cockily.

Brandon threw him a look and he shrugged nonchalantly and continued spinning his knife.

"As I was saying, the reason for this meeting is to finally end this long drawn out game of chess. We've put a real good hurting on the flow of business for Malik and his crew, but they are still operational and that's a problem. As you all recall, we had a bad bust due to a rat. A rat that is no longer an issue for us anymore. However, we still need to step up our game."

"So what does that mean?"

"It means that we have to stop focusing on the little fish and start targeting the bigger fishes. By bigger fishes, I mean the lieutenants."

Devon nodded and said. "It's about time. I was getting tired of these small timers."

"Bring on the gains," said Brock agreeing.

Brandon was glad to see that everyone was on board, so he wasted no time laying his new plans out on the table. The one man that was able to get info to Malik was dead. Malik no longer had an inside man, which meant he was blind now and that was going to work greatly in Brandon's favor.

"Everything in life has an order. Every business has a pyramid. In this business, there's the Kingpin, his trusted right hand man, the lieutenants and then the street goons. That's it in a nutshell. I'm sure that you all can identify between the small fish and the big fish."

Everyone gave their own form of acknowledgment and Brandon continued.

"In order to get to the top guy, we'll have to take out the people by his side... the middle men. That will leave him open and vulnerable."

Take out the king. That's how the game of chess is played. Brandon smiled at his plans. It was his best one yet and he was sure that it would be successful.

"Vladimir has been keeping an eye out on the areas that we've hit already to make sure that no one has backed tracked. They haven't been using the houses again, but Vladimir was able to tail one of Malik' street lieutenants and found out where another one of their stash houses is. Tonight I want Brock, Devon and Vladimir to check out that spot. Arrest anyone associated with Malik' crew."

"Just to be clear," Devon spoke. "You just want an arrest?"

"Yeah. One of those weak links will start yapping once we throw the book at him. I'm sure we will get a few names of the street lieutenant from them and once that happens, we can take them out and keep moving on up the chain."

"Hell, that sounds like a plan to me. I'm always down to cause some mayhem." O'Malley smiled and flipped both of his knives closed.

"And you will get your chance sooner than later O'Malley. In the meantime, I need you three to get a move on. Once we get what we need we can start digging up anything we can find to stick it to these muthafucka's."

All of the men nodded and proceeded to exit the room. Brandon stayed behind. When the room was completely empty, he pulled his cell phone from his pocket and checked the message that came in while he was speaking to his team. It was from Laila. A beautiful woman he'd met a few nights ago when he decided to visit one the nearby bars for a drink. She said she wanted to see him and asked when he could come over.

Brandon smiled at the message. He had been feeling on edge with everything that has been going on and Laila's message had come at a perfect time. He imagined having her chocolate legs wrapped around his waist while he fucked his frustrations away. That thought alone made his dick hard.

He licked his lips as he recalled the night he had seen Laila sashay into the bar wearing a dress that hugged her body so well it made every man in the bar stop and stare, including Brandon. The first thought that ran across his mind was that it should've been illegal for a woman to have that many curves. A woman like that needed to be fucked really good, at least that's the message Brandon received from her demeanor. She clearly knew what she was doing when she entered a bar full of men dressed the way she was dressed.

Brandon wouldn't mind having a taste of that chocolate, but he wasn't in the business of competing for pussy, so he decided it was time to call it a night. When he waved the bartender over to pay his tab, he was told that it was already taken care of. The bartender nodded towards Laila and then passed Brandon a piece of paper that had her name on it with her number. He did one better and gave the bartender his card to pass to her.

Although he didn't compete for pussy, he wasn't going to pass up a fine piece of ass either. Yet, calling a woman first meant she was in control and nobody controlled Brandon. If she wanted the dick she was going to have to ask for it.

Brandon looked down at the text again and smiled cockily. "Women are some weird creatures. Always trying to play games. I knew she would hit my line. They always do."

Brandon decided he would take his time responding back. He placed his cell back into his pocket and started to leave the room, but an eerie feeling made him stop in his tracks. Something wasn't right. Brandon walked back towards the head of the room where the podium and large projector screen were located. He checked the openings of the podium, but didn't see anything inside of it.

Ever since he found out about the rat, he had been on the alert and looking at everyone with a skeptical eye. He couldn't have another issue like that happening again. He couldn't afford to make another mistake and have his Sergeant pull him from his team.

Brandon surveyed the entire room, checking under the seats where his men had sat and the ones that were never occupied. He checked beneath the table and behind the American flag that stood in one corner of the room. He even checked the few pictures that hung on the walls. He looked up at the light fixtures in the ceiling squinting as if he could stretch his vision enough to see if there was anything out of the ordinary. Suddenly, Brandon started laughing. He shook his head and looked around the room once more.

"This shit has me losing my damn mind."

Pulling out his cell phone, he quickly sent Laila a message letting her know where to meet him.

~~~~

Malik was cruising down Bergen Street with his right hand man Nasir by his side. They didn't have an actual destination in place. Malik just wanted to clear his head and felt that a drive with his boy would do the trick.

Nasir was not only his right hand man and best friend, but he was also the one that helped Malik to keep a cool head so he wouldn't make fucked up decisions that he would later regret. The narcs really left a bad taste in his mouth and his trigger finger was rather itchy.

He'd lost some really good men these past few weeks. Men who had families and used the money they made working for him to take care of house and home. That was something he could never forget or forgive. Malik wanted revenge, not just for himself, but for the men who lost their lives too. *I'll make sure they didn't die in vain.*

"So what's the move?" Nasir asked, pulling Malik away from his thoughts. He was looking down at his phone texting, so he never noticed the fire burning in Malik's eyes.

Driving slowly, Malik was scanning the streets as they cruised through one of his busiest areas. "The cameras are in place and now that we have eyes everywhere, we'll have a better chance at finding out who these niggas are. We'll track em' down and then it's lights out," said Malik. His tone was flat, yet deadly.

Nasir sent his last text and then looked up just in time to peep some chick with a fat ass walking by. "I sent some of our men over to the old spots that got knocked to see if anyone was lurking around there."

"A smart man wouldn't back track," said Malik before stopping to let two kids with a ball cross the street.

"Well, let's just hope for our sake that these narcs got a few dumb asses in their crew."

"When I find out who is behind this shit, they're going to wish they never spoke my name. I'm gonna make their final minutes the worst few minutes of their entire life. Slow and painful. My face will be the last thing they see."

"Fucking pigs." Nasir felt the same as Malik. He grew up with a few of the men that had gotten killed. He wouldn't hesitate to pop a cop. All he needed was the go ahead.

"If any of them know anything about these streets, about this lifestyle, then they should know that fucking with a niggas money is an automatic bullet to the dome. Whomever is in charge of their team has to know that they will eventually be found. These fucking narcs step around here like they're some sort of Gods or something. None of the other real niggas that came before me wanted to do anything about this, but I damn sure plan to."

"I feel you on that one Malik. Just say the word."

Nasir's phone started ringing. He answered after the third ring.

"Talk to me. Uh-huh. Are you sure? Send it to me and chill." Nasir ended the call and glanced at Malik. "I guess our luck came sooner than we expected."

Malik cut eyes quickly over at Nasir before returning them to the street. "Yo' what you talking about? Who was that?"

"That was one of our men that I assigned to watch over The Pit. He said that a dark blue Lincoln has been parked across the street from the house for the past three hours."

"Ok, so what? Plenty of people leave their cars there to run tricks."

Nasir shook his head as he swiped through his phone and pulled up a pic to show to Malik.

"This ain't no regular trick, though. What nigga you know in our hood that looks like this? Dude must be Russian or some shit. He doesn't look like no regular white boy."

Malik pulled over by the park and leaned over to see Nasir's phone. "Looks like he has some people with him too."

"True dat. It's hard to make out their faces in this pic though," Nasir said, staring hard at the photo.

Malik took the phone to get a better look. He tried to zoom in on the other two people in the car, but it just made the pic blurry.

"Tell dude to keep watching them. Wherever they go, he goes and he doesn't return until he locates where one of them bitches lay their heads."

He looked at the picture again, a sinister grin crept across his lips. He knew a guy who had skills with face detection. He made a mental note to pay his old friend a visit and cash in on that IOU.

Malik dropped Nasir back off at their main house and made a quick trip home. When he got there, he turned on the sixty plus inch smart TV that he had mounted on the wall of his living room and reviewed some of the footage from the cameras.

He checked out each location, making sure nothing was out of the ordinary. When he saw that everything was flowing normally, he felt slightly at ease and headed to his room to change out of his street clothes. He reached into his closet and pulled out an Armani suit.

His old friend wasn't some regular Joe. Where he was heading, you had to know people who knew people and look the part too. There was no room for error. Street Malik had to be put on ice for a few hours so the civilized Malik could do his thing.

CHAPTER 17

"If you keep this up, I'm going to start assuming that dinner, a movie and monthly trips out of town will be next."

Brandon tugged his pants up over his boxers and re-buckled his belt. "You would be assuming wrong too. You know what this is."

Laila sat up and stretched her slender arms up over her head as she yawned. The thin white blanket that once covered her Double-D breasts now lay crumpled up around her waist. She reached for the half burnt roach in the astray that they both had been puffing on earlier and lit it again. She took a few tokes and offered it to Brandon.

"Lighten up Daddy, I'm just messing with ya."

Brandon eyed Laila's beautiful breasts and licked his lips. Just a few moments ago, her chocolate nipples were doing the tango with his tongue as he sucked and nibbled on them. He accepted the roach that Laila had offered him and took a couple of drags before passing it back.

"You weren't playing. I already told you what time it was. If you're looking for a boyfriend, I'm the wrong candidate."

Ignoring his response, Laila crawled across the bed, balanced her weight on her knees and pulled his face to hers. She traced his lips with her tongue, then turned her head slightly to the right and looked at him with raised brows. Brandon parted his lips and stuck his tongue out. She sucked it into her mouth and held the back of his head as she kissed him slowly.

Brandon reached around her and grabbed a handful of her soft ass. He couldn't resist Laila no matter how much he lied to himself about it. He would never tell her that though. In his mind, a woman was only what a man made her believe that she was. That's why he made sure that she knew that she was nothing more than a nice piece of ass. He would have never put up with that bullshit she was talking a few seconds ago from anyone else. But because he took a real liking to her, he let it slide this once.

Brandon smacked Laila's ass hard enough to make her squeal. He then grabbed a hand full of her braided hair and pulled her head back.

"My dick needs attention."

A devilish grin crept over Laila's pretty face. She reached for Brandon's belt that he had just not too long ago buckled up, and undid it again. She unzipped his zipper and slid her hand into his boxers.

Brandon shivered when the softness of her hand connected with his hardness. He palmed the back of her head and pushed her face closer to the part of him that ached for her mouth. Laila went to work; slobbing and bobbing. Sucking and deep throating him so good that Brandon almost felt like he was floating. He closed his eyes and enjoyed the feeling of every nerve ending opening up in his body. She was submissive, beautiful and gave good head…she was definitely a keeper. At least for the time being. Brandon's toes started to curl and his knees weakened as he got closer to his climax. He held a tight grip on Lailas' head as she continued working his dick.

"Damn, just like that," he told her and lolled his head back. He could feel the cum building up and makings its way to the tip of his dick. He braced himself for the large nut he was about to release. Just as he started coming his cell phone rung.

Cut It by O. T. Genasis played loudly and he knew that it was one of his men. Brandon stared at the phone until the ringing stopped, he told himself that he would call whomever it was back, but that notion was cancelled out when his phone started buzzing again. It was the same number.

"Wait a minute," he said while pushing Laila's head away from his crotch. She reached for him again and he swatted her hand away. "Chill out for a second. I gotta take this call."

Brandon adjusted himself and moved over to the window. "What's going on?"

"Sgt, we have movement at one of the old spots we raided."

"Are you sure it's them?"

"I'm positive. We got photos. I'm sending them to you now."

Brandon's phone vibrated twice. He pulled the phone away from his ear and looked at the screen. He opened the message that came through and smirked.

"That's those bastard's alright. Listen, call the rest of the crew. I'll be there shortly. Nobody moves until I get there."

"Roger that."

"You have to go so soon?" Laila pouted after he hung up the phone.

"Yeah, I have to handle some things."

"Will I see you later?"

"Maybe," he said while securing his body vest. He placed his service gun in the small of his back and pulled his windbreaker on over it.

Laila climbed down from the bed and walked over to him. She helped him adjust his gear and kissed him on the cheek before telling him to be safe. Brandon rushed down the stairs and out the front door. He glanced at the time on his wristwatch. *7p.m.* There was no time to waste. It was now or never. He was so close to bringing down his filthy brother that he could taste the victory on his tongue. The end was near.

~~~~

"Has anyone come out yet?" Brandon asked O'Malley as he peered through the set of binoculars that Vladimir handed him.

"Not since I called you."

"What's the plan?" Brock asked from the back seat of the car.

"We wait to see where they go next," responded Brandon, still looking through the binoculars. "Something tells me that this is a distraction to keep us off of what they're really doing."

"Do you really think that? I mean, these guys haven't been secretive about anything they've been doing since we started this mission. Their crew seems arrogant as if they truly believe that they are untouchable."

"Well, they're in for a rude awakening aren't they?"

Brandon turned his attention to his men. They were all piled up in an SUV that Vladimir had parked perfectly out of sight from others, but made sure that they had a good view of the house.

"I have this gut feeling that they're up to something. This spot is a decoy. The moment they leave we will follow them and I guarantee that they will lead us to the jackpot."

O'Malley, Vladimir, Brock, Zane and Devon all looked at one another, each having thoughts of their own about Brandon's gut feeling, but neither said anything. Brandon had more Intel about this mission than either of them possessed. He had proven that. They just hoped that this gut feeling of his didn't land them in another shitty mess like that house raid that flopped.

~~~~

After his meeting with his contact, Malik headed back to the headquarters feeling like he was ready to make some heads spin. His guy reviewed the footage from the tapes and was able to clean it up just enough for Malik to see that the man from the picture that Nasir had text to him was one of the men in the video.

His contact informed him that it would take him no more than twenty-four hours to clean up the other faces and run a search on who they were. Malik had no choice but to wait. He thanked his guy and went on about his way. With every second that passed he became more anxious.

Money, business, and family is how he viewed the world. One thing he hated more than anything was for someone to interfere with the flow of his business because that stops the flow of his money. And that shit won't be tolerated.

Malik pulled into his parking space and sat in the car for a few moments to calm himself down. He had already hit up his right hand man, Nasir, telling him to meet him here as soon as possible. Yet, he didn't see his boy's car.

He exited the car and made his way into the secluded warehouse. He walked through the large room of naked women cutting and bagging up merchandise with no interest what so ever. None of them looked away from what they were doing or said a word. Malik made it clear that he didn't want any of them speaking or looking at him. He couldn't risk one of those bitches selling him out. Just to be safe he made each one of them take a small hit of his fine merchandise twice a day so that they were able to still function, but too high to care about their surroundings.

One of the men guarding the room rose to his feet when he saw Malik coming his way. He quickly moved towards the enclosed staircase and pulled the metal gate door open for Malik to pass through. He offered a respectable head nod as Malik took to the steps.

There was another metal door at the top of the stairs with two more men were standing guard. One opened the door for Malik and then they both greeted him with a head nod as he walked up to the big double doors where his office resided.

"Let me know when Nasir arrives," was his only orders to the men before he disappeared beyond the doors.

Inside Malik was furious. His cool and calm demeanor was beginning to fade away and the old Malik was creeping out. He had replayed in his head many times how he would bring a slow and painful death to the muthafuckas that were tearing his shit down. Time was of the essence and he was certain that once he started peeling back caps, a lot of muthafuckas were gonna be regretting life.

Nasir finally arrived thirty minutes later.

"Yo, where the hell you been man?"

"My bad B, I was taking care of something and didn't notice your message right off."

"What was more important than you showing up here on time?" Malik looked Nasir up and down. "Something you need to tell me Nasir?"

Shaking his head at his boy, Nasir said, "Man it was just a lil' stop I had to make and straighten something out. We can talk about that later. Tell me what happened with ya mans and them at that meetup."

Malik looked at his friend as if he couldn't understand a thing he had just said. *Was this nigga serious?*

"So you're giving me orders now? You tell me what's important enough to discuss and what's not? Nasir you're my main man and everything, but don't get shit twisted. I give the orders and you execute them."

Nasir was no bitch and he knew that Malik knew this too. He'd put fools in the ground just for looking at him wrong. If he didn't have so much love and respect for the nigga he would have put one in Malik a long time ago. Nasir and Malik had been rolling strong together for years and he had never been spoken to like that before.

Although Nasir wasn't feeling the disrespect that Malik was throwing at him, he understood that his boy was on edge. Nasir decided to just let this one ride, but he told himself that it would be the first and last time Malik would ever speak to him like that. Next time, there wouldn't be a next time. Disrespect was not tolerated with him no matter who it was.

"You know what I meant by that."

Malik shook his head and sat on the corner of his desk. He realized that he was taking his frustrations out on the wrong person.

He meant what he said, but he wasn't proud of the delivery. "Yo, all of this shit just got a nigga real heated right now. I'm ready to put a muzzle on these muthafuckas that's all. My bad."

"It's cool," said Nasir, letting the shit go.

"My contact is scanning the video footage as we speak so I should hear something by tonight."

"Speaking of which, some of our men went back to one of the old spots to remove a few stashes from the walls and they said that they noticed some narcs watching them from across the way."

"Must be those same bastards from the tapes. Where are they now?"

"Waiting for my order to move."

Malik started pacing his office. He was thinking about what he should do. He contemplated whether he should wait until his contact sent him the information or have his men move to the next location. He continued pacing around the office fighting with his thoughts.

"A Malik."

"Hold on man, let me think."

"Nah, listen I just got word tha-."

"Nasir chill man, just give me a minute."

Nasir walked over to Malik and forced him to look at the screen of his cellphone.

"Read it."

Malik stopped pacing and read the message.

Narcs are gone.

"You see? Everything's good. I'll tell the men to move out quickly and watch their six."

Nasir could see Malik starting to relax a little. Before leaving, he made sure that Malik was straight and assured him that he would go to the new spot and make sure that everything was good.

~~~~

"Sergeant it looks like they turned down that alleyway up ahead."

"Yeah, I saw the bastards. Vladimir, give it just a little more gas. We don't want to lose their trail."

O'Malley leaned over the seat. "This is a different area, unlike their usual locations. Where do you think they're heading?"

Not taking his eye off the road, Brandon says. "I'm not sure, but we're about to find out."

They followed the men for another half a mile and ended up at an old abandoned shipyard. They all sat in silence as they watched the muscle car, full of Malik's men, drive through an opened gate and stopped shortly after. The back passenger door pushed open and one of the flunkies emerged from the car wearing baggy black jeans and a sleeveless t-shirt. The guy jogged back towards the entrance of the gate and pulled it close. He retrieved a chain from the ground and attached it to the gate to lock it.

"I knew my gut was right. I told yall they were up to something."

"So what's the plan now?" O'Malley asked, He was sitting in the back seat with both knives in hand.

"We know where their new location is now so it's time to do a house call."

Devon spoke as he peered out the tinted window. "How sure can we be that they don't have any other men in there?"

"Look around the gate. There's no security. That's a clear sign that they aren't expecting anyone to find their location."

"But we did," Vladimir said in his thick Russian accent.

"I'm always ready to fuck shit up," said Zane. "I think it's long overdue. This has been a hell of a week for me and I am ready to make some people hurt and bank some cash."

"In that case men, load up and let's shut this shit down," Brandon ordered.

Each man dismounted the SUV and met up at the rear end of the car. Vladimir did the honors of opening the hatch door and they all picked their weapon of choice. Brandon gave them a few minutes to check their gear and then they all hopped back into the SUV.

"Vladimir, you know what to do."

"Gladly," he responded, smiling evilly.

He mashed on the gas and the SUV's engine roared as it sped towards the gate. Everyone braced themselves as the front end of the SUV collided with the gate, pulling its metal frame off the hinges. Still moving at full speed, Vladimir raced the SUV down the dirt road that showed previous tire marks from when Malik's men entered. It was almost as if they had left a breadcrumb trail just for them to come and toss up their whole operation.

"I guess these boys never got briefed on covering their tracks," said Brandon.

He noticed a building up ahead that looked like an old trailer. He smiled to himself because he knew that this was going to be the quickest shakedown that they would ever do. There was no security and there was only one way in and one way out. Brandon had Vladimir stop a few meters away from the trailer and they covered the rest of the way on foot.

"Vladimir and O'Malley come with me. Devon, Zane and Brock; I want you to cover the perimeter in case any of them tries to hop out a window. If I recall correctly, there were only four of them that got into that car. I'm sure the three of us can take them all out easy enough."

"Roger that Sergeant," said O'Malley, pulling his shades from the top of his head and down over his eyes. "Let's move."

"Alright men. You have your orders. Let's make this quick. Remember, watch your six."

Brandon, O'Malley and Vladimir took off in the opposite direction from the other men. They ran across the dirt lot and surrounded the door. Brandon gave a three count signal to Vladimir and O'Malley, then they kicked open the door and started shooting. Two of the men inside were sitting on the sofa playing video games. They were the first to be hit. The other two men took cover and started busting back.

"It's those motherfucking narcs again," one of them called out to the other.

"These niggas don't give up. Kill 'em!"

Shortly after that, bullets started flying again. Brandon took cover behind a file cabinet and tried to peek out to see where each man was hiding. He spotted one in the doorway of what seemed to be a bedroom. He gave word to Vladimir, who happened to have a better shot, and he took action.

Vladimir fired off a few rounds in the man's direction and waited for the guy inside to fire back. When he did, Vladimir sent one more round his way and it landed directly in the center of the guy's forehead. Grayish-pink matter painted the wall behind him as his lifeless body flopped to the floor.

"Oh shit!"

That panicked cry came from the last man that Brandon still hadn't been able to pinpoint yet.

"You got two options; surrender or die. It's up to you." Brandon called out.

A few silent seconds passed and Brandon assumed the guy was

thinking about his next move. Instead of emerging and surrendering, the guy shouted. "FUCK YOU," and sent more rounds their way.

"I'm tired of toying with this fool. Swap out with me, Sergeant," yelled O'Malley.

Brandon traded places with him and watched as O'Malley placed both of his guns up near his head as if he was praying. He then emerged from behind the file cabinet and started sending nonstop rounds in the direction that he thought he'd heard the voice come from. O'Malley shot and walked until he had emptied both clips. He stopped and listened for any movement. Instead, he heard nothing but silence.

Brandon and Vladimir waited by the door quietly. When O'Malley finally found the last guy, he was slumped over in the tub. He had been hiding in the bathroom. O'Malley pulled the man from the tub and let his body hit the floor. He was still alive.

"We got a live one here gentleman," O'Malley called out giving them the signal that it was safe to enter.

"Good," Brandon said, walking up to the bathroom entrance. "Tie his ass to a chair and grill him. Do what you must."

O'Malley looked down at the injured man. "Your ass is mine."

Brandon and the other men began probing the rooms in search of any money or drugs that the men had stashed inside. Meanwhile, O'Malley had moved the injured man from the bathroom to the center of what would be the living room. He had him tied tightly to the chair while he questioned him.

"I'm gonna ask you once more…where is your headquarters?"

The man looked up at the ski masked covered face that was leaning towards him. Drenched in a mixture of sweat and blood, he panted heavily. The pain from his wounds was etched all over his face. "I'm telling you man I don't know."

O'Malley shook his head. "Wrong answer."

He drilled one of his sharp knives into the bullet hole on the man's right leg. When the guy screamed out in pain, O'Malley howled like a wolf and laughed hysterically.

"We found about eighty grand and a shit pile of blow," Zane reported.

"Well would you look at that?" O'Malley said sarcastically turning his attention back to his prisoner. "You boys must be putting in some major work in order to end up with loot like that. You look too dumb to even know how to run anything by yourself."

O'Malley circled the chair and pulled a second knife from its sheath. "Listen, I'm in such a great mood today that I am willing to give you one final chance to tell me what you know."

Beat down and weak, the man struggled to lift his head. "Please man, I really don't know. I've never been there before. None of us have."

"Is that your final answer?"

"Man, I swear I don't know."

"I guess you've left me with no choice." O'Malley looked over at Brandon, who nodded. No words were needed. Brandon, Zane, Brock and Vladimir gathered up what they had found and left the trailer.

When the door closed behind them, O'Malley frowned down at the man in the chair, flipping his knives in both hands. "This is going to hurt...a lot."

The painful screams of a man being carved alive was all the other men could hear as they walked back to the SUV.

CHAPTER 18

Brandon and his crew shut down another one of Malik's houses. Nothing made Brandon smile harder than knowing that he was the reason for his own brother's demise. After they stripped Malik's men of all of their cash, they waited outside in the car for O'Malley to finish turning one of Malik's men into a carved turkey.

Brandon had seen the damage that O'Malley could do with his knives and it wasn't an easy act to watch. In all of his years being in law enforcement, Brandon had seen many things occur. He had stood witness to all sorts of horrific scenes, but none of them topped watching a man be carved alive.

This may seem like a successful mission for Brandon and his men, unfortunately their fortune would also become their misfortune. They never realized that they were being watched the entire time. There was no security at that particular location because Malik had rigged the place with enough cameras to see every inch of the inside and outside of the trailer. No room or corner was left without video surveillance.

~~~~

"A creepy ass looking Russian named Vladimir Fedorov. A red hair, bushy eyebrow faced bitch name Chris O'Malley and a wannabe thug nigga named Devon DeMamp!" Malik slammed the manila folder that held the information of each man on his desk. Pissed off was an understatement.

"You mean to tell me that these are the fuck boys, that's been hitting my shit up?"

Nasir sat in the chair in front of Malik's desk in silence. He knew that was a rhetorical question. He just was waiting for Malik to finish tripping so he could hit him with more bad news.

"How in the hell did these mark ass niggas get by us with this shit? Seriously man I need to know. All that tells me is our security isn't worth two cents if niggas like this are slipping through the cracks right under our own noses."

Nasir looked on as Malik blew off steam and continued on with his rant. When he finally went over to the mini bar in his office and poured himself a glass of Rémy, Nasir decided that it was time to lay the bad news on him.

"Yo, Malik."

Malik stood with his back turned to Nasir. He looked over his shoulder, but said nothing.

"I got some more information for you and it ain't good man."

Silence.

"When I left from here, I went over to the new spot to check things out and make sure them little niggas was doing what they were supposed to be doing. When I got there the gate was torn from the hinges and there were several tire marks in the sand. I heard gunshots the minute I rolled through, so I parked my ride in the darkest area I could find.

A few minutes later I saw about five niggas running towards an SUV that was parked a little down the block. They were carrying our cash. They killed all of our men, and tortured Country bad.

I checked all the hiding spots for the cash and everything was empty. They cleaned the house out, but luckily they didn't fuck with the computer. I searched the tapes and saw their faces." Nasir reached in his back pocket and pulled out the USB he was carrying. He placed it down on Malik's desk.

Malik said nothing yet again as he walked over to his desk. He retrieved his MacBook from one of the drawers and powered it on. He placed the USB into one of the ports and waited for the video to open up. He skimmed through until he saw some activity and watched from there. Nasir sat off to the side, watching him. He knew that once Malik saw what he needed him to see, he was going to go off the deep end.

Twenty minutes into the video, Malik was leaned back in his seat watching everything unfold. He recognized the red head and the Russian right away. They seemed to be with another guy that he couldn't see because his back was turned.

Malik watched as the unknown man gave orders to the red head and the Russian. He was obviously the one in charge. The six mini screens on the laptop all lit up at the same time from the gunfire that started the moment the three men kicked open the door.

Malik watched as his men were taken down one by one. The unknown man was taking cover behind a file cabinet and looked like he was talking to the one man in Malik's posse that was left standing. Then the red head stepped in and started busting as he moved through the house. Moments later, Malik saw three other men come rushing in with the Russian. He recognized the Devon dude, but the other two weren't familiar.

The mini video screens showed the men scouting the house. Malik sat up abruptly in his chair when he recognized who the unknown man was in charge when he happened to look in the direction of one of the cameras. He replayed that part of the footage and slowed it down so he could get a better look at the guys' face.

His heart just about stopped beating and he felt a large lump in his throat as he tried to swallow the doubt that he felt. He shook his head and looked away from the screen. He had to have been seeing this shit wrong. It just couldn't be.

Malik stood up and walked over to his bar again, grabbed the entire bottle of Rémy, and drunk deeply from it. He knew that what he had just seen was a mistake. It had to be. He paced around the room a bit and looked over at Nasir, who looked at him and then shook his head as confirmation that Malik's eyes weren't deceiving him.

This can't be real. Maybe there was a glitch that screwed up the image and made him look like that. Malik slowly walked back over to his desk and replayed that part of the video again, but it was the same person. It was him. It was his baby brother. His own blood. It was Brandon.

Nasir watched the anger and hurt etched in Malik's face. He knew that a million and one questions were running through his mind. A million and one questions that needed a million and one answers. Malik was the kind of man that never let anything go unhandled. Situations like this is where the uncivilized Malik would resurface. Once that side of him showed up, that was it. No one ever knew their fate or when it would happen. He was always swift with it and by the time a target realized anything, it was too late. However, this was different. This was his baby brother. A brother that he loved and cared about.

Nasir cleared his throat to gain Malik's attention and asked the inevitable question. "How do you want to do this?"

Shaking his head, still in disbelief. Malik held up his hand, he needed time to think. But Nasir knew that time was limited and if they planned to do anything they would need to do it now.

"Yo, Malik man. I know you're upset, but we gotta handle this now. Just tell me how you want everything to go down and it's done."

"No." Malik closed his eyes and tried to fight back the tears that started to whelm in his eyes. He knew that Nasir was right, but he wasn't about to allow him to do anything to his brother. If anybody would handle Brandon it was going to be him. "You do what you must with the others, but leave him to me."

"You sure about that? I know he's your..."

Malik raised his hand. "I don't need a reminder. Take care of the others and leave *him* to me. He is off limits, understood?"

Nasir nodded his response and stood up to leave. "I'll let you know when it's done." He walked towards the double doors and knocked twice. The men standing guard on the outside opened the doors and Nasir walked out, leaving Malik to his thoughts.

~~~~

Brandon and his men were all in the conference room discussing their recent hit. They had scored big and now they were all ready to reap the grand prize...taking down the *nest*.

"I still feel like that shit was way too easy. They had to know that we were still surveilling their old spots. I mean, come on ya'll. You really think these guys just randomly picked that last location?"

Devon was sitting at the end of the table leaning back in his seat. His size thirteen feet were covered with steel-toed boots that rested on the edge of the table. "They are up to something. For all we know they could know who we are and be putting a hit out on us."

All the men looked at each other. The room was quiet for a few minutes until someone burst out laughing, causing a domino effect amongst the rest of the group. Devon shook his head in frustration at the reaction that his team members responded with. All the men laughed and cracked jokes, but not Brandon. He actually took in what Devon was saying and realized that he could be right.

"I don't find anything funny," he interjected. The laughter ceased and all eyes were on Brandon as he stood at the front of the room. "We shouldn't take anything lightly. Most of us have families that we care about. Our next move is to bring these thugs down permanently and in order to do that we must all have our heads in the game. Until that happens, it would be best for all of you to send your wives and kids somewhere safe until this is over."

"You don't really believe this crap do you?" O'Malley asked.

"A man can never be too careful," answered Brandon.

"I'm not about to make my family pick up and leave because of a "maybe" situation." Brock frowned. "I've been their protector all this time and I'll continue to be that. They aren't going anywhere."

"I can't make none of you do anything, but I will say this. You all better be ready for shit to hit the fan because this final bust is going to be big. I'm sure they are preparing themselves for anything right now. They may or may not know who is responsible for their loss of business, and we won't give them time to figure it out. We have to move fast. You got 48 hours to prepare and then it's go time."

Brandon left the conference room before any of the men could argue anything else. His mind was occupied with what Devon had said. Was it really a setup or another distraction to knock them off track from what was really happening? Brandon had no clue what was brewing, but he was going to make sure that he and his men were prepared for whatever was coming their way.

As he passed through the precinct in route to his office, Brandon realized that it had been quite some time since he had seen or spoken to his mother. He knew that she was always willing to engage in any conversation that involved his brother Malik. Brandon planned to pay his mother a visit that night and find out what he could about his brother's movements.

~~~~

Finally the work day was over and Brandon was more than ready to get home and shower. He hadn't eaten all day and could use a nice hot home cooked meal. He changed into a plain white t-shirt, blue jeans and a baseball cap before heading out to his mother's house.

The ride over there was faster than normal. It was as if everyone on the road could feel his hunger pains and decided to clear a path for him. When Brandon arrived at his mother's house he parked in the driveway and made his way to the door. He was greeted by the aroma of collard greens, macaroni and cheese, BBQ chicken and something that smelled like pumpkin spice.

When he entered the kitchen, he spotted his mother standing over the stove, stirring whatever was in the pot. She was dancing along to the music that played from the small radio that sat on the counter. He eased up behind her and grabbed her waist.

"Hey, Ma." He kissed her cheek and smiled at her surprised expression.

"Oh my gosh Brandon! You can't be sneaking up on me, boy. I'm getting too old to be surprised like that." She then turned and gave him a wide smile. "You showed up just in time, though. The food is almost done. You hungry?"

"Am I? I'm surprised the loud growls of my stomach didn't give me away before I made it over to you."

His mother tapped him playfully on the arm and laughed. "Why don't you go and relax until everything is done. I got some pound cake on the table if you need something to hold you over until the food is ready."

"Ok, Ma." Brandon went over to the kitchen table and grabbed himself a slice of cake then headed to the living room. He sat down on the sofa and grabbed the remote. His mother didn't mention anything about his brother coming over. *That was a good sign. I'll have her all to himself to find out what I can.*

CHAPTER 19

Malik's mind was heavy as he made his way to his mother's house. He kept replaying the footage of his brother over and over in his head. He couldn't believe that his own flesh and blood could betray him like that.

Ever since Brandon was a kid Malik made sure he was taken care of. He didn't want his little brother having to want for anything and he made sure of that. Malik spent every waking moment grinding hard for his family. He upheld his responsibilities as the man of the house to the best of his ability, but Malik suddenly came to the realization that Brandon had always been an ungrateful bastard. He never appreciated anything Malik ever did for him. He never so much as said a simple thank you.

Back then Malik thought it was Brandon's way of coping with the loss of their father. Maybe as he grew older he came to realize how much he really missed him and didn't know how to channel that frustration. Either way, Malik still didn't know how he planned to handle this issue.

As he turned on the street where he grew up and came to a stop outside of his mother's house, he spotted Brandons' car in the driveway. Malik turned off his car and sat there a few minutes more to gather his thoughts and calm himself down. He glanced over at the glove compartment that housed his Dessert Eagle pistol and contemplated if he would need it.

He shook his head to ward off the thought of ever harming his brother. He could never hurt him. However, the anger he felt was strong and the need for answers overpowered his common sense. He unlocked the car door and stepped out into the cool evening breeze.

When Malik entered the house he spotted Brandon in the living room watching the ESPN channel. The faint sound of music was coming from the direction of the kitchen and he assumed that his mother was probably back there dancing and cooking. He decided to take that moment to confront his brother.

Malik walked into the living room and sat down in one of the recliners opposite of the sofa, and looked at his brother. Brandon frowned as soon as he saw Malik. He didn't bother acknowledging him. He just kept his eyes glued to the television and tried to ignore his presence. He could feel Malik burning a hole in the side of his face with his eyes and it was annoying the hell out of him.

"Is there a problem, *Malik*?"

"I don't know *Brandon* you tell me."

"I'm not the one staring you down."

Malik looked Brandon over and noticed he was wearing a new gold watch. "Looks like life as one of New Jersey's finest is treating you well."

Brandon looked down at his watch and smiled cockily. "I have no complaints."

That pissed Malik off.

"I guess that's the new wave these days huh? Using stolen money to go on shopping sprees."

"That's a good question, you care to answer that one?"

Malik slid closer to the edge of his chair. "Check this, aight? I'm tired of fucking around with you Brandon. I'm trying to give your simple-minded ass a chance to fess up and return my shit."

Brandon nonchalantly sat back and crossed his left leg over his right. "I'm curious to know what you *think* you'll be doing to me if I don't oblige you."

"You keep playing games and you'll find out."

"I'm sorry, is that a threat?"

"Take it how you want."

Just then Gloria entered the room.

"I thought I heard another voice in here," she said, smiling as she started across the room to where Malik was sitting. As she got closer she noticed the deep frown on Malik's face and her smile changed to a look of concern. "Malik, baby, are you ok?"

Malik ignored his mother's question and continued the stare down with his brother.

"You're a joke," said Malik.

"And you're a lowlife wanna be that will never amount to anything."

"This coming from the punk ass officer who steals from his own brother."

"That's detective to you bitch."

"Hey, whoa. Now watch your mouth Brandon. What's going on in here?"

"Nah, Ma. He already thinks he can do whatever he wants. He thinks that whack ass badge makes him untouchable. I'm only gonna tell you once more to return what belongs to me."

"And if I don't return whatever it is that you think I have, what do you plan to do?"

"Brandon, what did you take? What's happening with y'all?"

"Don't push me, Brandon."

"Or what Malik? What are you going to do? I don't care who you portray to be to those lowlifes out in the streets, but you better remember that you're talking to an officer of the law. I can and will lock your dumb ass up. Now, threaten me again motherfucker!"

"Brandon what has gotten into you? Somebody better get to talking and tell me what is going on before I raise hell up in here."

"Ma, stay out of it," said Malik. He didn't want his mother to get involved with his and Brandon's argument.

"Don't talk to her like that," growled Brandon. His eyes narrowing.

"Brandon, you really have no clue do you?" Malik shook his head in disgust.

"Is that so? Well, why don't you enlighten me," said Brandon with a sneer.

Malik knew Brandon was always trying to impress their mother with his bullshit accomplishments so he thought putting him on blast was the best way to go at him.

Malik gave him a half smile, half sneer. "Go ahead and let Ma know what kind of nigga you really are. That you having a badge don't mean shit."

Suddenly, a loud crashing sound took over the room and both Malik and Brandon looked in the direction of the noise. Gloria stood in the entrance with her hands on her hips. There was glass on the floor from where she threw a plate to get their attention. She looked at her boys with the same look she used to give them when they were young to let them know she meant business.

"Now that I have your attention, I would like to know why you two are in here bickering and carrying on like this."

"Your son seems to have a problem with meddling in business that doesn't concern him and stealing things that don't belong to him."

"Stealing? That's a funny word."

Gloria looked over at Brandon. "Brandon is that true?"

Without taking his eyes off of Malik, Brandon said. "Ma, it's impossible to steal from someone who was never truly the owner to start."

"It really doesn't matter what you say Brandon. I saw you and your crew. I know you're responsible for the raids and I got tabs on every last one of your men. They won't be an issue anymore because at this very moment my boys are taking care of those bastards."

"Are you admitting to an officer of the law that you are planning to kill other officers?"

"Malik, tell me that you're not serious," Gloria said looking at him. "You won't have those people killed, right?"

Malik didn't respond.

"See, Ma. There you have it. That's your real son. The one you *love* to praise. This lowlife, trigger happy piece of shit," Brandon said with a smirk. "I guess I missed the part where being a drug dealer and a murderer was a good thing. Nah, fuck you Malik. You ain't nothing but a wannabe King Pin. You ain't no better than the people you sell those drugs too."

Malik looked over at Brandon with complete disgust. "You know what? You've been a thorn in my ass since you were a kid," he said as he stood up from his seat, anger radiating through his body. His heart was racing and the rage he felt was growing stronger and stronger. "You got a whole lot of nothing to say, but the reality is that you are no better than me. All those years in college gave you book smarts, but when it comes to this street life, you're dumb ass fuck. You turn your nose up at me being a dealer, yet you wanna be me."

"Pops may not have been proud of the decisions I made, but he would have been understanding as to why I made them. I did what was necessary for us to survive. I kept you out of the hood and tried to keep you away from the street life so you could have a better chance. But you were a waste of time."

"You may wear that badge, but there ain't no honor in a damn thing that you do. A man takes responsibility for his actions. A boy makes excuses to justify those actions. Sound familiar lil' bro? Those are the words of a great man. A man who would despise you if he could see what you've become. You're nothing but a crooked ass pig and Pop would be doing somersaults in his grave right now if he knew about this shit."

"I know what I am. I've never denied it. I embraced it. You?! You claimed to be one thing and ended up being something else entirely." Malik huffed sarcasticly. "A detective that makes no arrest because he kills everyone and then turns in most of the drugs and keeps the money to split with his boys. Yeah. Real honorable," he said in disgust.

Brandon's face grew hot from embarrassment. He could see his mother looking at him with disbelief. As far as she knew, before this moment, Brandon was a stand up cop with many decorations and awards to show for it. He never let on what he did outside of that. Now the cat was out of the bag, he hated Malik ten times more than before. Seeing that look in his mother's eyes pained him more than anything.

In anger, Brandon dug his hand in his pocket and pulled out a large knot of money. He threw it in Malik's face and the bills sprung apart, scattering all over his lap and on the floor.

"What? You short on cash, bro? No money left to pamper that slut Terry? Here, take this and hit up your connect. I'll just run down on another one of your stash houses and get it back later."

Malik had enough of Brandon. He moved across the room so quickly that Brandon didn't even have enough time to block his face from the right hook that Malik landed. Brandon flew back into the chair in shock at first, then he snapped back to reality and charged Malik. They both fell hard to the floor, throwing blow after blow at each other. Gloria screamed for them to stop, but her pleas fell on deaf ears.

"You done fucked up now," yelled Brandon, as he tried to stomp his size thirteen boot into Malik's stomach. But Malik was too quick and rolled out of the way.

Hopping to his feet, Malik threw another right jab hitting Brandon in the ribs. Winded, Brandon stumbled back and fell over the couch. Malik went over and grabbed him up by his collar. The menacing look in his eyes and the snarl on his face was a look mean enough to scare the piss out of anyone, but Brandon was not phased. He began to laugh hysterically at how riled up his brother was at the hands of him. That made Malik even more heated.

He threw a few more blows at Brandon and released his grip on him. Brandon fell to the floor gasping for air. Gloria stood in the corner of the room still screaming, but Malik was in such a rage that he paid her no mind. He reached for the waistband of his pants, but his gun wasn't there. He remembered he'd left it in the glove compartment.

Looking down at the bloodied mouth of Brandon, Malik fought with his other self trying to gain control. If he hadn't left his gun in the car he would have finished the job. It would have been one swift pop to the head and lights out.

Looking down at his brother, all he could see was the kid he used to be. He knew that his father would have never wanted things to end this way. After all the years that had passed since his death, Malik still respected his father and tried to honor him the best way he knew how. Killing his brother would not only have his father turning over in his grave, but it would hurt his mother as well.

Frustrated, Malik growled and kicked Brandon. "You better be thankful you're my brother and be grateful Ma standing here!" He stepped back and walked over to where his phone lay on the floor and scooped it up. "Next time, there won't be a next time. Stay out of my business, Brandon. I mean it."

Malik staggered towards the front door and stopped when he saw his startled mother standing in the corner of the room with her hand over her heart.

"I'm sorry for disrespecting your house, Ma, but you needed to know."

With that being said, Malik walked out of the door and headed for his car. Once inside, he attacked the steering wheel in frustration. He had come very close to ending his own brother's life. He was glad that he decided to leave his gun in the car. It was nothing to pop a nigga who crossed him, stole from him or came up short on his bread. He'd done it plenty of times and slept like a baby afterwards.

However, when he was looking down on his brother in the house, he realized that he would never be able to live with himself or face his mother again had he killed Brandon. Walking away was the best decision he'd made. He just hoped that Brandon took heed to his warning.

CHAPTER 20

Brandon clenched his teeth in pain as his mother dabbed a cotton ball soaked with rubbing alcohol over the bruises on his face.

"I swear, the two of you are going to be the death of me one day. I just don't understand how two brother's can hate each other so much."

"No disrespect Ma, but none of this concerns you."

Gloria placed her hands on her hips and took a few steps back. "Excuse me? When ya'll fighting in my house and breaking up my belongings you made it my concern."

"Ma, please. I really don't want to hear all of this right now."

"All I'll say is this, whatever it is that your brother thinks you have of his, give it back. Nothing in life is worth losing your brother over. You are grown men. You should be able to work things out without having to turn to violence."

Brandon was irritated. He didn't care about his mother's words. He was already planning his revenge on Malik. He remembered how the mere mention of Terry's name got him all riled up. Brandon knew how much his brother loved that whore. She was his weakness.

After he was all patched up, Brandon turned to face his mother. "Look Ma, I'm sorry for fighting in your house and messing up your stuff. Whatever got broken I'll replace it. Now this thing between Malik and I, it's got to play out. You're right, we are grown and we'll handle this in our own way." He stood and wrapped his arms around her giving her a gentle squeeze. When he released her, she looked up into his troubled eyes.

"What's this about Brandon?" For some reason she knew trouble was brewing and it was more serious than she first thought.

Brandon stared at her long and hard, but then smiled. "Don't worry, Ma. I'll end it," he said and walked out the door, leaving

Gloria with a sick feeling in her stomach.

Once he got back to his car, the first thing he did was check his phone. He had a few missed calls from Brock and a couple text messages all from his other men. He already knew what they were calling him about. He knew Malik wasn't putting up a front when he said that his men were out handling business. Right now, they were the least of his worries. They were all specially trained officers and could handle themselves. His sights were focused on his brother. He needed bait to get Malik alone and finally do away with him once and for all. There was only one person he could think of that would make his brother drop everything. Terry.

Brandon had come up with several ways to make his brother disappear without a trace, but as tempting as those thoughts were, it would've been way too easy. He wanted Malik to suffer. He wanted to weaken and make him beg for mercy.

He now stood outside his brother's house watching Terry through their bedroom window. He noticed how big her belly had grown since the last time he'd seen her. If his brother only knew who the real father of that bastard baby was he wouldn't be walking around like he had all the power in the world.

Terry removed the clothes that she was wearing and changed into a robe. When she disappeared from his view Brandon took that as his opportunity to make his move. He already knew which part of the house she would be in so maneuvering wouldn't be an issue.

He walked around to the back of the house and found the trip box for the power. He knew that if the power went out and came right back on, the alarm would have to reset itself, and that took at least four minutes. That was more than enough time to take out the two men patrolling down stairs.

He removed the wire cutter from his back pocket and cut every wire in the box except the power. After learning that Malik had cameras around his drug houses, Brandon was sure that he probably had a few in his house as well. Once that was done, he pulled out a knife and stuck it into the electrical cable box and slowed the level down until it stopped all together.

Brandon looked up just as the inside of the house went black. He now had four minutes to get inside the house and Brandon rushed towards the back door and kicked it in. He could hear Terry's panicked footsteps above him as she hurried from her room, but he didn't make a move for the streps. He was on a hunt for the two guards.

He saw the first one as he stepped into the hall and since he was unaware of his presence, he quickly lifted his gun with a silencer attached. He popped him twice and caught the body before it hit the floor. He saw a door nearby and dragged the body inside. He pulled the door shut behind him and started his search for the next one.

The second man was by the front door, holding a flashlight while looking at the alarm box. Brandon eased up behind him and popped him once in the head, leaving him slumped up against the wall. He reached down, grabbed him by the ankles, and pulled his lifeless body into a small room.

"Malik? Baby is that you?" Terry was standing at the top of the stairs. When she didn't get a response, she came down slowly.

Brandon hid in the shadows and watched as she entered the kitchen still in her robe.

She searched the drawers until she found a flashlight and turned it on. "Malik?" she called out, swinging the light around the kitchen. Seeing it was empty she headed back the way she came.

"This isn't funny, Malik." She started towards the living room. "JB! Shawn!" *Where the fuck are they*, she asked herself. Those two idiots were always doing stupid shit and this time she was going to let Malik know she wanted new people at the house with her.

Bandon continued to wait in the shadows. As soon as her back was to him, the lights flicked back on and she looked down to turn off the flashlight. Brandon stepped out of his hiding place and quickly threw a pillow case over her head. Terry screamed and started swinging wildly with the flashlight, but Brandon dodged her attempts of hitting him. He snatched it from her hand and tossed it to the floor.

"Let me go! What are you doing? Oh my God! Somebody help me!"

Brandon didn't utter a word as he fought to restrain her. For a pregnant woman, she was strong. He had to make her be quiet, but he didn't want to knock her out because he knew that he wouldn't be able to carry her back to his car. He began moving backwards, dragging her into the kitchen. He spotted a dish cloth and saran wrap on the counter and had an idea.

Before removing the bag from Terry's head, Brandon used one

hand to pull out the face mask that he had stuffed in his back pocket. It took a moment to get it on with all the struggling she was doing, but he managed to pull it over his head. He then took the bag off Terry's head and forced the dishcloth into her mouth just as she was about to scream again.

It was weird, but the fear in her eyes made his dick hard. It was always something about the way a person looked when they questioned if they were about to die that made Brandon feel superior. He smiled behind the mask as he began wrapping the saran wrap around the bottom half of her face to keep the cloth in place. He grabbed her chin and made her look at him. Terry snatched her head to the side, pulling from his grasp.

Brandon took a step back and pulled a large knife from behind his back and held it for her to see. He pointed it towards her stomach and stared directly into her eyes. Without saying a word he placed one finger up to his mouth and gestured for her to be quiet. Then he pointed at the back door. Scared for her child's life, Terry nodded her head as her way of acknowledging his silent instructions and began walking towards the door.

When they made it back to his car, Brandon popped open the trunk and pointed at the inside. Terry began to sob and made muffled pleas for him not to make her get in there. Still not saying a word, Brandon slowly lifted the knife he was holding and pointed at the trunk again. Terry stared at him with pleading eyes. Brandon tapped the flat side of the knife against her stomach and pointed at the trunk.

Defeated, Terry climbed into the trunk and laid on her side. Brandon tied her hands together and then her feet. It was then that he noticed that she wasn't wearing any shoes and her feet were bleeding. He slammed the trunk shut and hopped in the driver's seat of the unmarked car. Brandon turned on the radio and increased the volume. Tupac's *Live and Die in LA* played loudly as he drove off into the night with Terry in the trunk praying for her life.

~~~~

Still wearing the mask, Brandon placed a plate with a peanut butter and jelly sandwich on it and a cup of water on the floor. Without speaking, he walked out of the room that he had Terry locked in. They were in Amber woods, an old cabin that used to serve as a boy scouts camping ground years ago. Brandon remembered this place from a previous drug bust that he did on some meth heads that was trying to run a lab out there.

Terry had been going nonstop all day yelling and cursing, swearing on her unborn child's life that when her man found her he would kill Brandon. She had no clue that Brandon was her abductor, but she swore he was a dead man walking. Brandon had grown tired of her screaming and went back into the room to shut her up.

"You have no idea who your fucking with!" she spat when he walked into the room. "I'm going to laugh while I watch my man slit your neck from ear to ear you punk bitch."

Brandon removed one of the gloves he was wearing and slapped Terry across the face so hard she stumbled backward and fell on the old rickety bed. The robe that she was wearing came undone, revealing her very round belly, full breast and clean shaven pussy. Oddly enough, seeing her naked made Brandon's dick harden. There was a rumor that pregnant pussy was the best pussy a man could ever experience in his life. Brandon unbuckled his belt and walked across the room.

"No! What are you doing?" Terry screamed as she tried to squirm away from Brandon, who had forced her legs apart. "I'm pregnant. Please don't do this."

Ignoring her pleas, Brandon unsnapped his pants and pulled them down. He stared down at her through the opening of his mask and watched her expression as he pushed his dick inside of her. Terry tried to fight him off, but he held her hands above her head and kept stroking. Her cries soon turned into whimpers and then moans.

It was no surprise to Bandon that she was enjoying being raped. He knew that Terry was a whore from the moment he saw her. She was always just a pawn in this entire thing. He never had any feelings for her whatsoever. When he felt himself getting ready to nut, he pulled out and forced his dick into her mouth. Terry's eyes bulged as she gagged and choked on his semen. After Brandon was done, he fixed his pants and smiled behind his mask as he watched Terry roll over to her side and vomit all over the floor.

"You a sick son of a bitch!" she yelled, spitting towards him.

Brandon smacked her across the face and motioned for her to stand to her feet. It took her a moment, but when she did. He hit her again. That second slap being a warning that he was in control. Terry immediately got the memo and didn't talk back to him again.

~~~~

Malik had spent most of the night in his office still pissed off about the fight that he had with Brandon. He hated that things had gone that far between them, but Brandon was asking for it. He had given him several warnings and he had ignored them all. The only thing that kept Malik from taking his brother out, was their mother. Her pleas for them to stop fighting brought Malik back to his senses and he knew that he needed to leave right away before he did something he knew he'd regret.

"A man, I'm heading out. Ya'll hold down the fort."

"No doubt."

Malik gave a head nod to the two guards that stood outside of his office doors and headed towards the stairs. When he made it downstairs, he told the men that were scattered about holding their weapons the same as he did the guards upstairs. He was escorted out by three of his men and they waited until he was safely inside his car with his driver before heading back into the building.

"Take me to my spot."

Malik leaned back in his seat and closed his eyes. All he wanted to do was get home to his lady and let her help him relax. The thought of Terry's soft body made his Johnson tingle. He reached down and readjusted himself and imagined how wet she would become right before he entered her from behind. He smiled, remembering how she never wanted him on top because she felt unattractive because of her pregnant belly. But Malik honestly thought that she was even sexier now.

The thought of him having his first child with the only woman to hold his heart, besides his mother, made him very happy. Every night that he came home to a sleeping Terry, he would just stand over her and watch her. She always looked so peaceful, skin glowing and smooth. Each time he did that, he thought about quitting the game, marrying her and then moving his family into a nice house where their baby could grow up safe. He knew that his father would be proud to see that new change in him. It couldn't erase his past, but it would surely be a start to a better future.

Almost thirty minutes later, Malik's driver pulled up outside of his place. He got out and gave the driver instructions to come back first thing in the morning. Then he made his way up the few steps that lead to his front door.

"Terry!" He called out to her as he dropped his keys on the small mail table that sat near the door. He removed his coat and hat and walked towards the kitchen. Malik opened the refrigerator and grabbed a cold beer. He popped the top off and took a long swig from the glass bottle.

"Yo T!" He called out to her as he exited the kitchen and headed towards the stairs.

He started up the steps and could hear the sound of water running from the bathroom. Assuming that she was in there, Malik walked up to the bathroom door and tapped on it lightly.

No response.

He pushed the door open and found that the shower was running, but there was no Terry. Confused, Malik walked down the hall to their bedroom and found that it was empty too. He started to feel a bit of anxiety as he pulled his phone from his pocket and dialed her number. Her line went straight to voicemail. This wasn't like his girl to leave and not tell him anything. She would always call or text him to let him know where she was. Malik then realized that he didn't recall Terry ever calling him to see when he would be home and that was also not like her. Thinking the worst, Malik dialed Nasir's phone.

"One."

"Yo, Nasir I need you to meet me at the crib ASAP."

"Malik, you good?"

"Nah nigga, Terry is missing."

"I'm on the way."

"Call some of the hitters and have them come too."

"Say no more."

Malik paced back and forth wrecking his brain trying to figure out where Terry could be. She didn't have any friends so he knew that she wasn't hanging out. She stopped hanging with them as soon as she found out she was pregnant. Her family was pretty much nonexistent in her life, so he doubted that she was with any of them.

She probably made a run to the store and her phone died or something, Malik thought as he continued pacing around their room.

Suddenly, he heard his phone going off. He stopped and sighed with relief. Assuming that it was probably Terry he didn't even look at the caller I.D.

"Yo baby, where you at?"

A sinister laugh came through the phone. "Awww, you thought I was your bitch?"

"Who the fuck is this?"

"I have something you want."

Malik didn't recognize the voice on the other line. It sounded like the person was using one of those voice disguisers that made them sound like the guy from the *Saw* movie. At that moment, several thoughts coursed through Malik's mind and he immediately wondered what it is that this person had that he'd want.

"I'm listening."

"Good, then you shouldn't have a hard time understanding these simple instructions. You have 48 hours to come up with ten million dollars or the person you love most will be nothing more than a memory."

"Ten million? Man listen, I don't know who you are or what games you're playing, but you got the wrong muthafucka. The only thing you'll get from me is this lead I'mma put in ya if you don't stop playing on my fucking phone."

Malik ended the call and walked over to one of the bedroom windows to see if Nasir and his men had arrived yet. He didn't see any cars outside and cursed under his breath.

"Where the fuck is this nigga?"

His phone rang again and he answered immediately.

"Yo' Nasir, where you at?"

There was a muffled sound on the line at first, then the panicked screams of a woman came through. Malik's heart just about stopped beating when he realized that that screaming woman was Terry.

"Terry?!"

"Have you ever heard the screams of someone having their teeth extracted without being drugged first?"

Malik stood rigid with fury. "Don't you fucking touch her!"

"Here, let me give you an example."

Terry screamed again and begged the person to stop. Hearing his girl being tortured and not being able to do anything about it pissed nearly drove Malik insane. He knew that he would have to comply with this bastard to protect her.

"Alright man, I'll do it."

"I knew you would come to your senses. Ten million. Forty-eight hours or each minute that you delay your girl will lose a tooth or maybe a toe. Don't show up at all and well... Maybe I'll help her deliver your little boy. It is a boy right?"

Malik shook his head and tried to keep himself together. He needed to go along with what he was asking so he wouldn't hurt Terry, but in the back of his mind he was already planning out a way to find and kill him.

"How will I know where to drop the money?"

"Wait for my instructions."

The call disconnected and Malik stood in his bedroom feeling a little defeated. That moment was short lived when he recalled the way Terry had been screaming in pain. All he could think about was her and his unborn child. He had to come up with a plan and fast. Then another thought crossed his mind. He didn't recall disarming the alarm. And where the fuck is JB and Shawn?

Malik headed towards the stairs and began a search of every room. He found both of his men dead from shots to the head. He checked the security cameras and saw that the feed had been cut. *Fuck.*

"Yo' Malik! Malik you in here man?" Nasir and six other men entered the house all strapped and ready for war. "Malik!"

Malik slowly walked back into the living room and snarled at Nasir.

"What the fuck took y'all muthafuckas so damn long?"

Nasir turned his head to the side and looked at Malik as if he had lost his mind. He could have sworn that they had spoken previously about the way he shouldn't talk to him like he was some punk nigga. Nasir took a step forward, ready to check him, but he realized that now wasn't the time due to the extreme circumstances.

"What? Am I talking to my fucking self?"

"Listen, I had to round up a few nigga's and as you can see, we're all here and ready for whatever. Just say the word."

Malik looked around the room at the faces of all six men and nodded his approval. "Ya'll chill for a minute and give me and Nasir a few minutes."

Malik walked away and headed towards the kitchen with Nasir not too far behind him. Once he felt they were out of earshot, he began to give Nasir the details about the call he received.

"He's asking you for ten million within forty-eight hours or he's going to kill Terry?"

Malik nodded.

"You got a clue who this person could possibly be?"

Shaking his head slowly, Malik said, "Nah, not even the slightest. Hell, they knew I wouldn't be home around this time, because I was at my Mom's. Either they know me or they've been watching me."

Nasir thought for a few seconds. "You think this some kick back from one of those cats we jammed up?"

"Nah, those lil' muthafuckas ain't that damn smart. Whoever this is must have been planning this shit. They knew where I lived and they disabled my security cameras, maybe even my alarm system. They even was smart enough to disguise their voice over the phone. This person has some type of personal beef with me and when I find out who it is, I'm taking his ass out."

"So what's the word?"

"We wait for him to hit me back with his instructions and then we make our move from there."

CHAPTER 21

Malik poured himself another glass of Rémy and started pacing the room again. He had been waiting for the last three hours to receive a call from the mysterious voice. Within that time, he had been thinking and trying to figure out who could have been behind this.

His gut was telling him something, but he couldn't pinpoint what it was exactly. He looked around the room at all six of the men who were scattered about either standing or sitting. He couldn't help but wonder if any of them had anything to do with Terry missing. Any one of them could have been some type of spy or a snitch.

Malik pondered that thought as he continued to look at each of them one by one. The longer he looked at them the more he realized that his thoughts were just that, thoughts. None of them were smart enough to do anything like that or dumb enough to fuck with him or his family.

Feeling satisfied that it wasn't none of his boys, he left the living room and returned to the kitchen. Nasir was standing near the window talking to someone on the phone, but as soon as he noticed Malik he ended the call. That made Malik's suspicions kick into full effect. He wanted to know who it was that Nasir was speaking to and why he ended that call so abruptly.

Terry's missing was starting to make him view everyone differently. He was beginning to realize that he'd turned a blind eye to things that he should have handled—like the time when Nasir called himself checking him because he chewed his ass out for showing up late at the spot.

Malik even recalled another time when he caught Nasir throwing a menacing look his way when he gave him orders to take care of something. Actions like that would usually get a nigga popped, but he didn't allow himself to react in those moments. Instead, he made it clear to Nasir who was in charge and kept it pushing.

As he stood in the kitchen looking at Nasir, he couldn't help but wonder if he held a hand in his Terry's disappearance. After all, he was Malik's right hand man. Hell, Nasir was the one who linked Malik up with the firm who hooked up his security systems for his home and his drug spots. He found it odd that the person who took Terry knew exactly how to disarm his systems and maneuver around his crib without getting picked up on the cameras.

Malik had cameras that came with a backup battery so his spot would have 24 hour surveillance no matter what happened. Those cameras came in handy a while back when they had to evacuate the city due to a possible storm. The power in the neighborhood was out for two days and there had been complaints about people breaking into houses. Someone broke into Malik's spot and stole his TV and a few other electronics. When he returned home, he viewed the tapes and recognized the thief. Long story short, he made it so that muthafucka' would never be able to steal anything again by chopping his hands off.

Malik was convinced that this was no coincidence and that it was an inside job. He boiled over with anger on the inside, but managed to keep a calm appearance. The murderer in him wanted to rear his ugly head and start busting on niggas, but if he allowed himself to get to that point he knew that he would never find his lady.

"What's up man?" Nasir asked as he slid his phone in his pocket.

Malik threw a head nod Nasir's way and leaned against the kitchen island counter.

"Nothing. Just trying to keep a cool head."

"I feel you," Nasir said as he smoothed his hand over his head. "I've been calling in favors from some people who owe me. I got some men putting in footwork and keeping their ears to the streets for anything they could find out that would tell us where Terry is."

"What's the status with those cops ya'll tailed?"

"We got them chilling."

"Details."

"I had some of our men tail them and watch their every move. We caught some footage of them pocketing the drugs and money that they got from some of the busts they did on our spots. They know that we have that and at any given time we can release it all over the news. They all fell back. They got too much to lose, feel me. So in a nutshell, we made them our bitches. Anything you need, they will do."

Malik was still suspicious of Nasir, but he couldn't resist feeling impressed with the work that his boy had put in. He had a few more men in blue in his pocket now and he didn't even have to pay them. He was impressed, but that wasn't enough to deter his feelings about Nasir.

"Good work on that. You need to get those bitches up and let them know we got a situation. We're going to need them to help us find Terry."

"Say no more." Nasir pulled his phone out and started typing something.

Malik's blood was running hot through his veins. He couldn't believe that he allowed a scumbag like Nasir to get that close to him. After all that he'd done for him, yet he goes and do some shady shit like this. Malik knew that this shouldn't have come as a surprise to him. This was how all partnerships in the drug game seemed to turn out. The right-hand man is always the one that turns out to be the biggest snake of them all. Malik recalled his father telling him once that he shouldn't be so trusting of people.

Only tell them what they need to know. It's always the ones that you allow to get close to you, who will hurt you most.

Those words echoed in the back of his mind as he tried with everything in him not to lose his cool. Nasir had been giving him signals all along. It was just fucked up that it had taken all of this to go down for him to realize it.

Just then Malik's phone rang. The words *unknown caller* lit up his screen and he instantly knew who it was.

"I'm listening."

The voice on the other end of the phone rattled off the location where Malik was to meet him to do the exchange. He scribbled those notes down on a crumpled napkin that was on the counter and passed it to Nasir.

"What's the word?" Nasir asked.

"Get all of the men together and have them at this location in an hour." Malik passed the paper to Nasir and walked away. The fat lady had sung and it was game on.

~~~~

Brandon placed the phone down on the table next to his gun,

leaned back in his seat and propped his feet up. The smile he wore on his face made Terry cringe. When she heard Maliks' voice on the other end of the phone she wanted to scream out to him, but Brandon had a gun pointed at her the entire time. Her face, eyes and lips were swollen from the beatings that Brandon had given her. She sat on a turned over bucket on the opposite side of the rickety table completely nude. Brandon had raped and beaten her every hour on the hour while cursing her and her unborn child. Everything pissed him off. If she so much as blinked in his direction, he would slap her across the face. Terry quickly learned that avoiding eye contact and only speaking when he demanded her to, was the way to avoid his wrath.

"You wanted to scream. I could see it in your eyes. I could also see that you were aware of the consequences you would be facing had you made that stupid decision."

Brandon stared at Terry. His eyes roamed over her bruised body and lingered on her large belly. A sinister grin spread across his face. All day long he'd been replaying the scene over and over in his head of how Maliks' face was going to look once he told him who the real father was of Terry's baby.

He had less than an hour to get her dressed and over to the drop off location. Before calling Malik, he had reached out to O'Malley, Vladimir, Brock, Devon and Zane to tell them about the meetup. They informed him of Malik's men running down on them, but assured him that they were still loyal to him. They wanted revenge and was down for whatever.

Brandon felt relief in knowing he could still count on them. After confirming that they were up to speed on his plans, he made the call to Malik. Brandon was no fool. Brother or not, he knew that Malik would have an army of his men somewhere lurking in the darkness just waiting for the perfect moment to take him out. That's why he made sure to stay several steps ahead of him and have his men set up shop at the location beforehand.

~~~~

Malik sat in his parked car enclosed in the darkness of the alleyway. He watched as his contact jogged across the busy street and looked both ways before making his way into the alley. He tapped on the passenger side window and waited for Malik to hit the button to unlock the door.

Malik did a subtle check of the surroundings to make sure no one had seen them.

"What you got?"

"Something heavy man."

Malik looked over at his contact. "Heavy?"

"All I'll say is that your instincts served you right."

With that being said, the contact removed a silver MacBook from the worn out backpack that he had in his lap and opened it up. He used his index finger to move the mouse around on the screen and clicked on a file. The screen went black for a few seconds and then another window popped up with video footage that showed the outside of Malik's house.

The first thirty seconds of the footage showed no signs of suspicious activity, then suddenly a man emerged from the tree lines that surrounded Maliks' home. Malik watched closely as the man stood on one side of the house looking up where the main bedroom window was located. He stood there awhile just staring in that direction, then he finally walked towards the back of the house and stopped at the power box that was attached to the wall. He removed something from his pocket and fumbled around with the box, then he made his way up the back steps and kicked in the kitchen door. Malik's contact fast forwarded the footage to the inside of the kitchen. No one was there.

"I don't get how this guy was able to bypass the camera, it's facing the door."

"Just wait for it."

Suddenly, the video glitches and the kitchen door that was just kicked in was back in tack and the broken glass was gone.

"Wait, what just happened?"

"Someone hacked into your security man. They froze the shot to make it look like everything was normal. Luckily for me, their skills aren't that great, because I was still able remove the bug and capture an image of the intruder."

The guy moved the arrow around on the screen again and tapped a few buttons on the keyboard. A second screen popped up with an image that automatically shuffled through several pictures of different people. After about twenty seconds, the shuffling came to halt at a photo of a face that was very familiar to Malik.

"I was able to catch his face as he kicked in the door, it was a bit difficult cleaning up the image, but I got it." The contact turned the computer towards Malik. "You know him?"

Boiling over in anger, Malik clenched his jaws together and nodded his response.

"Did you know that he was a cop?"

"Yeah."

"I did some more digging through the other videos that you sent me from your other spots. The men in those videos are cops as well and I learned that they all work for the same department." He pointed at the screen. "I'm no rocket scientist or nothing man, but I think you now know who has been responsible for all those busts."

Malik remained quiet. He couldn't believe that he hadn't put two and two together before about Terry. Instead, he began blaming his crew. It didn't matter at this point, because Malik had already decided that it was time to eliminate the problem. Brandon.

Noticing the dark look in Malik's eyes, the contact gathered his belongings and removed a thumb drive from his computer and passed it over to Malik.

"Can I have my payment?"

Malik picked up the Beretta that was resting in his lap and aimed it at the contact. "Back up."

"Yo man, what's up with this?" he said backing away.

"Back the fuck up!"

"Alright, alright. Be easy with that thing."

Once the contact backed away from the car, Malik took off down the narrow alley. His tires screeching loudly as he made a hard right turn back out into the street. His thoughts were racing a million miles a minute. The murderer inside him had resurfaced and he had a taste for blood.

~~~~

Malik arrived at the meeting point and parked in an area that would allow him to see his men, but not be seen. He waited a few minutes, then he pulled out his cell and dialed Nasir's line. The phone rung twice and he watched as Nasir pulled his phone from his pocket and answered.

"Yo."

"Where is he?"

Nasir looked at his watch. "He should be arriving any moment."

Just then Malik noticed a black suburban creeping up. He watched as the SUV pulled into a parking space a few yards up from where Nasir and his men parked and the driver's door opened. His heart nearly beat right out of his chest when he saw Brandon step out. He was alone. Or was he?

"He's coming your way," said Mailik. "But he doesn't have Terry with him."

Nasir looked around subtly. "Yo' you can see me? Where you at?"

"Stop looking around, just be cool and wait for my order when he reaches you."

"Ok."

"Be careful. This motherfucker might have something up his sleeve."

"Say no more. One of his boys already hit me and told me that they were here too."

"You got that in check, right?" asked Malik. He wanted to be sure those mother fuckers were playing for the right team.

"You already know."

"He's closing in on you. Look to your left."

As soon as Brandon reached Nasir, Malik told him to put him on speakerphone.

"Glad that you could make it, *bro*," Malik said, letting Brandon know he knew who was behind Terry's disappearance.

"I expected you to be the coward that you've always been and not show up." Brandon remained unmoved by Malik's absence.

"I was surprised to find out that it was you who busted up my spots. I always thought you were a pussy. I never took you for a go getter. Shit, kidnapping Terry was some shit I would have done myself. I definitely didn't think you would go against family, though."

Brandon laughed. "I guess this is supposed to be the part where I buckle over and have a change of heart right?"

"I'll let you decide that, bro."

With that being said, Nasir thumbed around on his phone, then held it at eye level in Brandon's face. Brandon was hesitant at first, but he looked at the picture and the cocky smirk that he once wore was slowly replaced with a deep frown. Malik watched from his car and smiled when he noticed how Brandon's body language changed.

"Now, as I was saying, you will meet me at my spot and you will have Terry or I share this information with your chief and every news station in this city."

"Nah, that's not going to work for me."

"I wasn't asking."

The phone line disconnected and Nasir and his men raised their guns at Brandon.

"Well, you heard the man." Nasir frowned. "And you can wave your boys off too. Yeah, we know they're here."

Brandon looked at Nasir like he wanted to try him, but knew he was out numbered and out gunned.

"Go ahead and try for it. Please," Nasir said in a deadly tone.

Brandon smiled widely and let out a light chuckle. "Nah. This round in yours. But, I'll be seeing you again." He turned around and waved his hands in the air to signal his men to stand down, then proceeded to his car.

CHAPTER 22

Malik pulled up outside of the warehouse and handed his keys to one of the guards out front.

"Park it in the back."

He then made his way inside of the warehouse and summoned all of his men to their makeshift meeting room.

"Listen up! I'm sure ya'll niggas done got wind that we finally found out who was behind the raids on the spots. That motherfucker is on his way over here now. He's a dumb mother fucka' so he'll probably call in for backup. I need ya'll niggas to prepare yourself for war. Shit's about to go down. Go suit up, load up, and take your positions."

Malik pulled a bogie from the pocket of his shirt and lit it. He took a few pulls of the cigarette and exhaled thick white smoke in the air. He remained where he was as he watched his men prepare for a fight. Seconds later, he felt his phone vibrating and saw Nasir's number come up on the screen.

"What's the verdict?"

"We followed him to some shitty ass cabin in the woods. He got Terry..." He paused a second too long and Malik instantly felt his heart beat speed up.

"He got Terry and what?"

"Yo, she don't look so good man. She looks like he's been beaten on her bad and he stripped her of all her clothes."

Malik removed the phone from his ear and pressed it on his forehead hard. He clenched his teeth and tried to compose himself around his men. That wasn't the news he wanted to hear. He couldn't imagine the thought of anyone ever raising their hands to his lady, yet it happened and he couldn't be there to do anything about it. He was going to make sure that Brandon regretted that.

"How long before ya'll get here?" he asked gruffly. His anger made his voice sound course.

"We about fifteen minutes out."

"Bet."

"Yo, Malik, I saw ol' boy chopping it up on the phone. He called his crew."

"I knew he would do that," Malik said, tapping the Beretta at his waist.

"That Devon nigga hit me up as soon as he called him. He gave them the location and time. He told them to come weighted down."

"You got that under control still, right?"

"Like a trick on the streets," said Nasir firmly.

"Good. If anyone of them pigs fold, dead they ass."

"10-4."

Malik placed his phone back in his pocket. He dropped the bogie and stepped on it as he started to make his way towards the gated stairs that led to his office. He told the two guards outside of his office that no one was allowed up there for any reason what-so-ever.

As usual, both men nodded their response and Malik disappeared beyond the double doors.

CHAPTER 23

Brandon kept looking up at his rearview mirror. Malik's goon's were following him. They had been tailing him since they left from the meet up. They didn't seem to be the smartest bunch when it came to it either, because Brandon spotted them right away. They were three cars back, but he could make out the guy who had handed him the phone earlier clear as day. He thought about losing them, but he didn't need them raising any awareness to Malik about anything. As soon as he returned to his car he called Brock and told him to get the crew together. He needed them as backup.

"I need ya'll to grab all the hardware you can find. We're going to need it if this thing goes left."

"What happened at the meeting?"

Brandon sighed and rubbed the bridge of his nose. "He had videos of us casing his spots. Everyone's face was visible. He even has footage of O'Malley when he..." His voice trailed off. "He threatened to release the footage to the press and the captain if I didn't meet him at his place."

"Dammit! That's the same shit he did to us."

"Look, I'm sending you the location and I'll hit you again once I make it there. We need to destroy that evidence."

"No shit. I'll round everyone up."

Brandon continued driving as he tried to come up with a plan. He knew that he couldn't just drive around, because they would know that something was up. So, he decided that he would return to the cabin. When he got there he saw that Terry was in the farthest corner of the room, curled into the fetal position. There was a pool of red fluid around her.

"Shit!" Brandon said as he rushed across the room to her. "Hey, wake up!"

Terry didn't move. He nudged her with his foot, but she still didn't flinch. Fear rose in his chest as he looked down at her lifeless body. He had no clue of what to do. The blood around her was a dark red color and he knew that couldn't be a good sign. He had only been gone for a few hours and before then, she seemed to be fine except for the few bruises on her face, arms and legs.

Brandon rolled Terry over on her back and placed two fingers against her neck to check for a pulse. He then tried her wrists and sighed with relief when he was able to find one. It was faint, but it was there. The dark red blood that was pooled around her reminded him that he had another problem on his hands, the baby. There was no way for him to get her to a hospital without Malik's men seeing him and reporting this back to him.

Brandon left the room and returned seconds later with an old blanket and a bowl of water. He cleaned Terry and put the same clothes he made her take off earlier, back on. He retrieved more water and made her drink some of it. He needed her up and able to walk out of the door so Malik's men could see that she was ok. After a few trips back and forth from the room to the kitchen, Brandon had gotten her hydrated enough to where she was able to open her eyes and be coherent.

"I need you to get up and walk. Can you do that?" he asked. Not waiting for a response, Brandon pulled Terry up from the floor and allowed her to place her weight on him as he slowly walked her to the door. She grunted in pain with each step and tried to stop a few times, but Brandon forced her to keep moving.

"Something's wrong with the baby."

"We don't have time for that right now. I need to get you in the car."

"I need to get to a hospital," she said panting heavily.

"You either make yourself find the strength to walk out of this door or you can find yourself buried alive out back. You choose."

Terry grunted and breathed in and out slowly as if she was trying to control the sharp pains in her stomach. She inhaled deeply and exhaled a few more times, then she stood straight up and nodded. Brandon opened the door and pulled his gun from the small of his back.

"Don't try anything stupid. I will not hesitate to blow the back of your head off."

Too consumed by the pain, Terry ignored his threat and limped pass him and out of the door. She held onto her belly with one hand and used the other to hold onto the rickety wooden rail as she took one slow step after another down the uneven stairs. When she finally made it to the SUV, she opened the door of the passenger side and looked back at Brandon.

"I'm going to need help getting in here."

Brandon hissed and place his gun in his waistband and helped her up into the SUV. Once she was inside, he closed the door and walked around to the driver's side and got in.

~~~~

O'Malley, Brock, Zane, Vladimir and Devon all stood together at the top level of a deserted parking garage. They were looking over a handwritten map that Brock had sketched out and was using to give the men a visual of where they needed to be located for Brandon.

"Are we sure we want to do this?" asked Devon. "They know where we all live and threatened to kill our families if we helped him."

"If it were you, wouldn't you want us to help you?" Brock asked looking up at him. "We are a team. We started this shit together and we're going to end it together. All of our asses are on the line, including yours Devon. They have video footage of us remember?"

He then looked over at O'Malley. "They have you carving that kid up like a Thanksgiving turkey on video too. With that kind of evidence floating around, we're all likely to lose the lives that we know. This moment right now would be the least of our worries if those videos are released."

Brock fished around in his jacket pocket and pulled out a black pack of D'jarum cigarettes. He patted the bottom of the pack several times before opening it and placing one on the tip of his lips. Vladimir offered him a light and Brock nodded his thanks as he took a long pull before exhaling.

"No one is safe. This is why we have to take them out and destroy any evidence they have on us. The Sergeant ain't the only one in trouble right now. We all are. And if we don't do this, we can kiss our happy little lives goodbye."

All of the men stood there silently thinking about what Brock had just said. They all were aware of the consequences if they stepped in to help Brandon. Nasir and his men had given each of them a chance to back away from this family feud. He'd told them that they were to speak to him and only him, if Brandon were to reach out with plans of taking Malik out. If they crossed Malik, Nasir had threatened to torture and kill each man's family while they watched.

No one spoke for a while, then O'Malley broke the silence.

"Well, since we're fucked either way, what's the plan?"

"We don't have much time to go over the specifics, so this is where you guys have to use your tactical instincts. Brandon is on his way to this location," Brock pointed at the address on the map and then pointed to a worn down warehouse building a few buildings away.

"We're less than five minutes from there. He's going to text me when he arrives to let us know what the perimeter looks like. Apparently, this place is the headquarters of this drug kingpin so be expecting lots of barriers. Once we get there we'll take out the men outside and make our way inside."

"Vladimir, I'm going to need you to find out where this guy's office is. You might run into a few of his men, but I know you can handle yourself. Zane, I need you to do that thing you do with explosives. O'Malley, just be the savage you are and Devon you will be our eyes just in case more of them show up."

"What if none of this stuff comes together as planned?" Devon asked while staring down at the map. "What if we're walking ourselves right into a big ass trap? One of those guys could be pretending to be the Sergeant just to see if we'll stick to the rules they gave us."

"I never thought about it like that." Vladimir scratched his head thinking.

"I guess we won't know until we get there, won't we?" Brock frowned. "Until then, just stand by for the Sergeant's orders."

Brock walked away, but he was also thinking about what Devon had said too. What if this was all a setup? There was no time to think about backing out now. They were all going to find out soon enough.

~~~~

Brandon kept his eyes on the rearview mirror as he waited for the light to turn green. He could still see Malik's men tailing him. Terry was sitting in the passenger seat moaning and groaning from the sharp pains in her stomach. She kept telling Brandon that she needed to go to the hospital, but he ignored her. They were minutes away from their destination and he'd already given Brock the heads up.

Brock replied back, letting him know that the team was very close and that gave Brandon a little relief.

The light turned green and Brandon proceeded down the street until he came up on an alleyway so narrow he had no choice but to drive slowly. He looked up and checked his rearview mirror again. No one was behind him. The further he crept down the alleyway, the more he started to feel uneasy.

The alley opened to a wide area that was enclosed by a crumbling brick wall. Up ahead was an old warehouse. Brandon counted about two snipers on the roof and approximately eight to ten gunmen patrolling the outside. He snapped a quick picture with his phone and sent it to Brock. As he drove up closer to the building, he heard one of the men yell for him to stop. Then three of them started walking towards him with their guns drawn.

"Get out of the car, slowly!"

Brandon looked over at Terry. He held her gaze as he slowly began to reach for the handle of the door and push it open. He whispered one last warning to her before exiting the car. The second his feet touched the ground, one of the men came forward and gut punched him with the butt of the rifle he was holding. Brandon heaved over and coughed. He tried to catch his breath and stand upright, but he was forced down by another hard blow to his stomach and a kick to his back.

"Yo!"

Everyone stopped and turned to the sound of the voice. Brandon regained his composure as Nasir parted through the men and came up to him.

"Not quite the welcome you were hoping for huh?" He waved at one of the guys to help Terry out of the car. He watched as she limped around the SUV and stopped in front of the car to lean against the hood. "You ok?"

Terry avoided looking at Brandon. "Yes, I'm ok. Where's Malik?"

"He's inside waiting for you." Nasir frowned at Brandon. "And you."

Brandon kept his game face on and said, "Well, let's get this shit over with then."

Nasir led the way to the entrance of the warehouse. Brandon, Terry and the other men followed along. Brandon appeared to be calm on the outside, but he was really hoping that his boys showed up soon.

CHAPTER 24

Brock, Vladimir, O'Malley and Zane were making their way to the location while Devon's voice crackled through the earbuds they all were wearing. He gave them a head count of the men who remained outside of the warehouse guarding the door.

"It looks like it's six of them. Three at the gate. Two by the door and one on the roof."

"You think you can take out that one on the roof?" Brock asked.

Devon adjusted the focus of his sniper rifle and aimed it at the guy on the roof. "I'm locked on him. What's your ETA?"

"We're rounding the corner as we speak."

"Just give me the signal."

Vladimir pressed on the gas and zipped around a few cars that were driving the speed limit. He followed the GPS until it brought him to a narrow alleyway. Slowing to a stop at the entrance, he looked over at Brock.

"GPS says it's up ahead."

Brock placed his finger to his ear and spoke. "Devon, we need eyes."

"Three still on the outside of the gate. They're holding AK's. The two at the door have shotguns."

"Do you see anything that can be used as a shield?"

Devon scanned the area through his scope. There was some debris that was scattered about. Some were tall enough to take cover behind, but it wouldn't be a good shield from bullets.

"It doesn't look good man. He picked the perfect place. It's a wide open lot with nothing to hide behind for cover."

Brock turned around in his seat and looked back at O'Malley and Zane.

"Well boys, it looks like we are going to have to charge our way in.

When Devon takes out the sniper on the roof, that will be our cue."

O'Malley flipped the knife that he was twirling one last time before placing it back in its sheath. "Roger that."

"Zane, you got the stuff?"

Zane patted the pack sitting in his lap. "It's all here."

"Good," said Brock nodding. "Vladimir, make sure you head in last. Make your way around the chaos and find that office."

"Got it."

Brock pressed his finger on his earbud again. "We're moving in."

"I got you covered." Devon's voice crackled back.

Brock, O'Malley, Zane and Vladimir exited the black suburban and made their way down the narrow alleyway. They stopped short of the exit and waited for their signal. O'Malley peered around the corner just as the silent round from Devon's rifle connected with the sniper's head. A pink mist was the only thing that was left of it. The other men turned to the sound of the sniper's body hitting the ground. Brock, Zane, O'Malley and Vladimir used that moment of distraction as their cue to attack.

Vladimir rushed out into the open with his guns drawn and took out the first guard with two rounds to his chest. O'Malley, Brock and Zane weren't too far behind as they began firing away. In no time all six of the men that once guarded the perimeter of the warehouse were dead. The team then regrouped and made their way to the entrance of the warehouse.

"I'm sure those shots alarmed them inside," said Brock as he wiped his forehead with the back of his hand and checked the magazine of his gun. "It's go time. Shoot to kill anyone that isn't the Sergeant. Understood?"

Everyone nodded in agreement. Zane pulled open the door and they all moved inside with their guns at the ready.

~~~~

Terry ran into Malik's arms the moment she saw him. She cried as he held her and told her that everything was going to be okay. He took a look at her and noticed the black eye, as well as the bruises all over her arms and legs. Her tattered and blood stained clothes made his heart race with anger. He couldn't believe that his brother could do such a thing to a woman. A woman with child at that. Malik touched Terry's belly and looked her in the eyes.

"How's the baby?"

"Okay, I guess, but I need to see a doctor," she said with concern in her eyes.

"Don't worry, I'll make sure I get you to one as soon as I finish here." He kissed her on the forehead. "Why don't you go on up to my office and wait for me."

Terry was escorted through the gated door that led to the stairs to Malik's office. When she was out of sight, Malik's eyes darkened as he turned his attention to his piece of shit brother.

"Tell me why I shouldn't blow your damn head off right now?" Malik asked Brandon.

Unfazed by Malik's threat, Brandon smiled. "Because if you do your bitch will be a single mother raising your bastard child without you."

One of Malik's men gutted Brandon with the butt of the rifle.

Brandon collapsed to his knees and coughed. He held his stomach as he tried to regain control of his breathing. Then a sinister laugh escaped his lips.

"Come on Malik, you know just as well as I do that we both have something to lose. You won't kill me because you don't want to spend a life sentence in jail." Brandon spat on the floor and stood up. "You wanted your bitch and I brought her to you. Now give me what you have on me and we can end this."

Malik shook his head from side to side. "Uh uh. See, it's not that simple anymore Brandon. You took things too far and there's no turning back now."

"Malik, you are really good. You know that?" Brandon looked around and smiled. "This act that you're putting on for these worthless pieces of shits. You may have them fooled with this thug shit that you're doing, but I know you. I grew up with you. I lived with you and I know that this ain't nothing but a big front."

Malik took slow and deliberate steps towards Brandon as he continued to rattle off insults. When he got close enough to his brother, he offered up a strong right hook to his jaw. Brandon stammered back and grimaced at the sudden taste of nickel on his tongue. He touched his mouth and saw that his fingertips were covered with blood.

"You better rethink your next move. These men right here are very trigger happy and would enjoy filling your body with hot lead," said Malik.

Brandon shifted his eyes over to the men that were scattered about the warehouse with their firearms pointed at him just waiting for the green light from Malik. He knew that he needed to calculate his decisions. He needed to keep things from going left before his team arrived. He spat out the blood that filled his mouth and wiped his lips on the back of his hand.

"You still hit like a bitch," said Brandon smiling. The blood had smeared all over his teeth, causing them to look pinkish.

"And you still don't have a clue of the way things work in this world, do you?"

"Look, you got what you asked for and now it's time for you to give me what I came for."

Malik nodded his head and drew in his bottom lip as if he was thinking about what Brandon had said.

"Damn. You're such a disappointment Brandon. We tried to give you a better life. Give you a chance to make something of yourself and you still screwed that up. Ma would be so ashamed."

"Man, please. You ain't did a damn thing except make my life hell. Everything that I got, I got on my own. Those college degrees and my career were all because of *me*. You don't get any credit for that shit."

Malik laughed and looked over at Nasir. "You believe this?" he asked, not expecting a response. "This dumb muthafucka' really don't have a fucking clue. You really think that you made it all those years by yourself?" he asked staring back at Brandon. "Nigga my name is what put fear in those lil' nigga's hearts so they wouldn't fuck with you. You got accepted to that school because I had a little talk with the dean. And don't forget who paid for all that shit. Oh, and don't get me started with the your job."

Malik had Brandon's full attention now.

"That's right lil' brother. I had some words with your Captain to help you land a spot in that precinct because that fat powder nose muthafucka owed me a favor."

"Every accomplishment in your life has been because of me. I set you up so you wouldn't fail and you managed to do so anyway. Me watching over you is how you remained safe, but no more. You ruined that when you betrayed me. If you know anything about these streets like you claim to, then you should know that stopping another man's money and interfering with his livelihood is a death wish. But the worst shit to do is to fuck with his family. You fucked up with that shit."

With those words being said, Brandon heard a gun cock and his eyes locked on Malik's right hand man Nasir.

"So this is the part where I die now?" he asked as he continued staring Nasir in the eyes. "Is the part where you have to get another man to kill me because you're too much of a coward?"

Brandon was doing well at keeping a calm outer appearance, but on the inside, he was beginning to panic, wondering where O'Malley, Brock and the rest of his team were. He was running out of time.

CHAPTER 25

O'Malley, Brock, Zane and Vladimir had taken cover behind a few stacks of crates that was pushed up against the walls of the warehouse. After taking out the guards out front, they made their way inside of the warehouse and took out the two men who were supposed to be watching the door. They could hear voices as they got closer to the main room. Brock was about to give the order for the ambush when he heard something that made him stop in his tracks.

Malik had made a statement that confirmed he and Brandon were blood brothers. That was news to him and judging from the other men's reactions, it was news to them as well. To make matters worse, they had also learned that their own Captain was involved in this fuckery somehow.

Brock began to put two and two together and realized that they were all Guinea Pigs in this so called "mission." A mission that Brandon conspired and the Captain approved of all for one reason; to kill the one person who could ruin their careers with the information he held.

Suddenly, Brock had a change of heart. He wasn't sure if he wanted to risk his life anymore. He wasn't sure if going against what Nasir had told them was a smart idea anymore. He was beginning to think that maybe Devon's paranoia wasn't an overreaction.

"Yo, Brock. What's the plan?" O'Malley asked, breaking his train of thought.

"I don't know. I'm not sure what to do right now."

"Did I really just hear that guy mention that he and the Sergeant were brothers? Did he mention the Captain's name too?" Vladimir asked. He was still trying to wrap his head around the news.

"Yeah, you did," confirmed Brock.

"As fucked up as all of this is Brock, I still say we go in there and finish the mission. We can deal with the Sergeant later, but we mustn't forget that we can go down too, if that information is leaked."

"I hear you O'Malley, but can't you see that we've been getting played this entire time? Who's to say that this wasn't preconceived. That the Sergeant and the Captain didn't set us up to case those houses knowing who they belonged to. How do we know that the Sergeant wasn't aware of those cameras?"

O'Malley shook his head in frustration. "Look, right now is not the time to try and analyze this shit. We're hiding behind some raggedy ass crates in a warehouse full of armed men who are unaware that we are here. We need to get through this ambush, get the shit we came for, and get out as soon as possible. We will deal with the rest later."

"I don't know about y'all, but I'm ready to blow some shit up," said Zane as he held up his pack.

Brock took in everything O'Malley had said and realized that he was right. Continuing with this mission wasn't just going to be to save Brandons' ass, but it would cover theirs too.

"Okay, let's get this done. But when this is all over, we deal with the Sergeant."

"Good to go."

"Roger that."

"Alright then, on me," said Brock as he stepped around the men and peaked through the crates to get a visual. He then raised his free hand and silently gave a five second countdown. He paused on one and glanced over his shoulder at the other men. They all nodded in unison that they were ready and then they formed a skirmish as they emerged from behind the crates firing round after round.

~ ~ ~ ~

Brandon was staring down the barrel of a Gold Magnum Desert Eagle desperately trying to figure out his next move. There was no sign of his team and he was starting to wonder if they'd backed out on him. He didn't have time to give that idea too much thought. He needed to figure how to get out of this mess.

"You got anything to say?" Malik asked. He was standing off to the side with his hands doubled together resting over the crotch of the designer jeans he wore. His expression was unforgiving and unsympathetic.

The silence in the room could be cut with a knife. Brandon started to say something when he heard a round whiz past his head barely missing him and hitting one of Maliks' men square in the chest. Everything seemed to slow down as he watched one man after another take a bullet to the chest or head and hit the floor. He'd thought for sure that he was going to be a dead man and had almost given up. He finally came to his senses of what was going on around him and charged at one of Malik's men who was trying to reload his gun.

Nasir was distracted by the unexpected ambush and had turned his gun away from Brandon and started firing at the attackers. Brandon tackled another man to the ground, wrapped his arms around his neck, and broke it in one swift move. He picked up the dead man's gun and started firing at the other flunkies. He fired until he had a clear path to make it over to his men.

"Glad ya'll could finally make it," he yelled over at O'Malley, who was off on his right firing away.

"Yeah, we ran into a little trouble."

The sound of gunfire had consumed the warehouse. Men were dropping left and right. Some dead; others badly wounded.

Brandon took cover behind some crates and scanned the room to locate the others. Brock was held up behind a wall having a shootout with Nasir. Vladimir had made his way around the warehouse and was squatting behind some more crates scoping out the staircase that led to the second level. Zane was shooting at Malik and a few of his men while he was planting explosives in different areas at the same time.

Brandon zeroed in on his brother, who was being guarded by his flunkies. Every time he tried to come up and take a shot at Malik one of the flunkies fired at him first.

"You niggas are going to die tonight!" Malik yelled. "Y'all picked the wrong muthafuckas to mess with. Kill them all!" he ordered.

More bullets flew rapidly throughout the warehouse. Zane fired back until he hit one of the men guarding Malik. O'Malley fired off several rounds while Zane took cover to reload his gun. When Brandon peeked out from his cover he saw that Malik's men were trying to get him over to the stairs that led to the second floor. Brandon yelled for someone to cover him as he emerged from the crates and took out two of the five men guarding Malik with fatal shots.

"Leaving so soon Malik?" Brandon called out from behind the crates.

"You're a dead man Brandon!" Malik yelled back. "You just don't know it yet!"

"We'll see about that."

Meanwhile, Brock was waiting for the perfect moment to catch Nasir slipping. Nasir was hiding out behind a metal pillar.

When Nasir showed up at Brock's place that night and threatened to kill everyone he loved, as well as ruin his career, Brock knew that he would have to kill him. He told Brock that Brandon had screwed over the wrong person and there was a price on his head. He warned Brock that if he or any of the other officers running with Brandon interfered that they would suffer terribly.

To prove his point he rattled off a few addresses that Brock instantly recognized and that was all he needed to hear to get the picture. Brock gave his word that he wouldn't involve himself, but he knew he couldn't abandon his partners. Now here he was in the middle of a shootout in some abandoned warehouse trying to take down the man who threatened his and his family's life.

"You can't hide forever mutha'fucka!" Nasir yelled out at Brock.

"Who said I was hiding?"

"I knew you wouldn't listen to my warning. You want to die don't you? Did you say goodbye to that family of yours yet?

"Only person dying here tonight is you."

"I doubt that," Nasir said as he came from behind the metal pillar and started shooting his way over to Brock. Brock came up to send some bullets back and was hit in the shoulder. He retreated and slid down to the floor grabbing at his shoulder. He grimaced as he pulled the neck of his shirt down to check his wound. The bullet had gone clean through.

"That's only a small fraction of what I plan to do to you," Nasir called out. He had moved from his original spot and was now crouched down behind some crates that weren't too far away from where Brock was. "What's the matter? Cat got ya tongue bitch?"

Brock remained where he was. He ripped the sleeve off his shirt and did his best to use the ripped material as a temporary bandage. He wanted Nasir to keep talking so he could get the drop on him. It was as if someone was on his side, because while Nasir was running off at the mouth, he backed into the crates and gave away his position.

Brock stood up with no hesitation and fired at those crates until his clip was empty. There was no movement for a while, but Brock wasn't taking any chances. He listened closely until he could hear the sound of someone gasping for air. With his gun still drawn at the ready, Brock took slow and deliberate steps towards the fallen crates that once stood as Nasir's cover. When he looked over the crates, he saw that Nasir was lying flat on his back wheezing and grabbing at his chest. The shots hit him twice in the chest and once in the leg.

Brock grimaced down at the dying Nasir and kicked the gun lying next to him to the side. Removing a fully loaded clip from the pocket of his cargo pants, Brock reloaded his gun, cocked it back and aimed it at Nasir's head. His eyes were bulging out of his head as he still tried to breathe. Brock showed no sympathy as he pulled the trigger. The wheezing stopped instantly and Nasir's body lay lifeless on the cold concrete floor.

Malik was being guarded by his men as they made their way to the stairs that led to his office. "Malik! Malik are you ok?" Terry yelled from the entrance of the stairwell.

"Terry, go back upstairs!" Malik yelled back to her. "You and the baby don't need to be down here right now."

"I was worried about you."

"I'm good. Now go back upstairs!"

Just then Terry screamed. Malik turned around to see that Brandon had Terry in a choke hold with his gun aimed at her head.

"Brandonnnnn! Let her go!" Malik growled and pointed his gun at his brother. His men had their guns turned on O'Malley, Zane and Brock. No one noticed that Vladimir had slid into the caged stairwell and had made his way to the second floor. The men up there had been taken out during the shootout, so he didn't have any issues finding his way to Malik's office.

"This bitch right here?" Brandon smiled evilly and shook his head. "No can do my brotha. You see, I would have enjoyed nothing more than to just kill you and be on my way. But somehow there's a higher being on my side that made it possible for me to make you suffer first."

"I should have blown your fucking head off when I had the

chance."

"But you didn't because you are nothing but a coward. Had to get your man to do your dirty work. You know where he is now?" Brandon nodded his head and looked in the direction where Nasir's lifeless body lay.

Malik followed Brandon's eyes. His jaws tightened in anger when he saw that Nasir was dead.

"I have never been one to do a lot of talking, but due to these circumstances, I think it would only be fair to tell you the truth before you die." Brandon nudged his gun into the side of Terry's head so hard that she screamed. "You care to tell my dear brother our secret?"

Confused, Malik looked at Brandon and then at Terry.

"Terry?" Brandon nudged his gun into the side of her head again. "Go on tell him."

"What is wrong with you?" she cried. "You're sick!"

"Not as sick as Malik will be. Now tell him bitch!"

Terry kept her red and tear-stained eyes down to the ground. "Brandon, please stop this."

Brandon cocked his gun and said. "That wasn't a request."

Malik had all his attention focused on Terry. It was obvious that something was going on that he didn't know about. "Tell me what, Terry?"

Terry shook her head as if she was trying to wake herself up from a bad nightmare. Malik called her name again and she just about passed out.

"Malik, I'm so sorry."

Even though he hadn't heard her reason for being sorry, he felt his gut tighten and anger began to resurface. "Sorry about what? Tell me what's fucking going on."

Terry cried and felt sick to her stomach. She couldn't believe that she was about to tell her man, the love of her life, the most devastating news that he would ever hear. She wished that she could take that gun that Brandon held to her head and kill his conniving, crazy ass with it. The longer she lingered the more the news would cut deep, so she took a deep breath and looked Malik in the eyes.

"This baby...is...isn't yours."

"What? Whose is it then?" he asked through clenched teeth.

Terry dropped her eyes again. Malik stared at her and then at

Brandon and back at Terry again.

"Nah." He shook his head. "Tell me that you aren't saying what I think you're saying."

Terry just cried. "Malik, I love you baby. I'm so sorry. This was all a mistake. I wish I could take it back, but..."

There was a loud bang and time seemed to stand still for a moment as everyone stood looking in shock at what they'd just witnessed. When Terry's body hit the ground, Malik felt like his breath had been knocked out of his body.

"As I said, I was never one for too much talking," Brandon said nonchalantly.

"You son of a bitch!" Was all Malik could muster to say before he started blasting at Brandon. His men followed suit and started shooting at the other officers as they all ran for cover.

"Brandon, you're dead." Malik continued firing. Each time he pulled that trigger, he kept seeing Terry's body fall to the floor.

"I thought you would be more appreciative that I helped you see that bitch for who she really was. She was an unloyal whore."

Malik had taken cover behind one of the metal pillars. He had his eyes fixed on the crates that Brandon was hiding behind. They both knew that only one of them would walk away from all of this, but they were both determined that it wouldn't be the other.

"There's no need to prolong this dance Malik. I'll tell you what, if you give up, I'll make your death quick and painless. What do you say?"

Several bullets went flying in Brandon's direction.

"That wasn't quite the response I was looking for," he said with a chuckle.

They shot back and forth at each other until both of their clips were empty. Malik stepped out into the open and summoned for Brandon to show his face.

"Guns are for pussies. We can settle this the old fashioned way."

"I'm not a little kid anymore Malik. This won't be like that time when I was running smack for Vice. And Ma ain't here to stop us. This time I'm going to kill your ass."

Malik gestured for Brandon to follow through on his threat. Brandon removed his vest and his duty belt. He let those items fall to the ground as he walked towards Malik. He balled up his fist and took a fighting stance smiling at Malik enticingly.

"I'm gonna make you pay for killing my girl and my baby."

"I can see I'll have to beat some sense into you. That was my baby, bro."

Malik charged at Brandon and swung, missing his head by an inch. Brandon moved out of the way just in time to come back with a hard kick to Malik's right leg. That hit caused Malik to lose his footing for a second, but he recovered quickly and came back with a left hook that caught Brandon square in the jaw.

Brandon tried to grab Malik into a headlock and they tussled for a while until Malik was able to break free and throw more punches Brandon's way. Brandon got some jabs in as well, but none of them were hard enough to stop the raging storm in Malik. He was out for blood and his only mission at that point was to beat the life out of his brother. He had betrayed him and killed the only woman he loved. The only calm to Malik's storm would be to hear Brandon take his last breath and he intended on making that happen.

"I'm tired of playing games with you," Brandon said as he wiped the blood from his mouth. He then pulled a knife from his ankle revealing it's large blade and dared Malik to try him.

"Weak men fight with weapons."

"And pussy's cry over dead bitches."

Brandon swung his blade and it caught Malik's shoulder. He stumbled backwards, grabbing at his arm. He grimaced at the instant pain it caused. His fingers were painted with his own blood, but he didn't let that stop him.

When Brandon tried to cut him again, Malik charged him and tackled him to the ground. The hard impact knocked the wind out of Brandon and his knife went sliding across the cemented floor. Malik held Brandon down with his weight while he delivered hard blows to his head. When Brandon tried to block the blows to his head Malik moved his punches down to his chest and ribs.

With blood dripping into his swollen eyes, the disoriented Brandon managed to block one of Malik's blows and hit him in the temple. That impact made Malik roll off of Brandon and by the time he was able to shake it off, Brandon had already scurried to his feet and picked up the gun belonging to one of Malik's dead men. He stood over Malik and aimed the gun at his head.

"You should have gone with my first offer," said Brandon as he popped off a single shot to Maliks' leg. He knew he could have just as easily killed him, but for now he just wanted to keep him down.

"You're weak. You've always been weak," Malik said unphased by the gun that Brandon was aiming at him. "You always wanted to be like me. You wanted my life. You wanted my girl. You envied the respect that people gave me. I guess you think that by killing me, you'll be able to take control." Malik laughed. "You will never fill my shoes bother, no matter how hard you try."

"You really think people respect you, huh? I bet you think those muthafuckas over there respect you too."

Malik spat at Brandon's feet. "If you're expecting me to beg for my life, then you might as well stop wasting time and pull that trigger."

"You're still trying to put on for these simple minded niggas?" Brandon asked and looked at Malik's men, who were all on the floor with their hands behind their heads. "You think they'll give a damn about you once you're gone? I guarantee that every one of those bitches would jump at the chance to drop a dime on you just to save their own asses."

Malik shook his head as if he felt sorry for Brandon. "Loyalty. They're loyal to me and I'm loyal to them. That's how respect is developed. Loyalty is a word that you will never know the meaning of."

Brandon did an imitation of Eddie Murphy's infamous laugh and said. "I thought he was going to say something worth listening to, but he sitting here with a gun pointed at his head talking about shit that makes no sense." He laughed again and became serious. "Are those your last words?"

"I'll see you in hell."

"Yeah? Well, you'll be waiting a long while. No worries though. I'll let Ma know that you won't be home for dinner."

Brandon squeezed on the trigger and shot Malik in the chest. He watched as his eyes bulged as he fell over on his side, wheezing and grabbing at his chest.

"That's the look I wanted to see." Brandon stood over his dying brother and smiled evilly. The look of defeat on Malik's face was priceless. "Sleep tight, bro." He pulled the trigger once more sending a bullet between Maliks' eyes. He exhaled with satisfaction and walked away.

"As for the rest of you niggas, you have two choices…die or work for me." He cocked his gun and aimed it at the first guy. "Choose."

Each man knew that Brandon wasn't fronting about killing them, so they all agreed to work for him.

"Good. Now get the fuck out of here and remember, I know where you stay. I know where your families stay. If a word about tonight gets put to anyone, you and yours will join that muthafucker," he said pointing his gun towards Malik lying in a pool of blood.

"Whoa Brandon, what are you doing?" Brock asked. "You do realize that you just let four eye witnesses go free?"

"They won't talk," he said confidently.

"So, what...we just risked everything to come here and you just decide to pull some shit like this? What? We're supposed to be drug dealers now?" asked Brock.

Brandon pressed up against Brock until he backed him into a wall. "You got something that you need to get off your chest? You're questioning my authority?"

"I think I said exactly what I needed to," responded Brock.

"Maybe it's you who I need to be paying close attention to," Brandon retorted.

There was a brief stare down between Brock and Brandon. They looked like they were ready to go to war with one another and add two more bodies to the ones they left in the warehouse.

"Uh, guys?" Zane intervened. "We really don't have time for this. We have about ten minutes to get the hell out of dodge before the bombs I set go Ka-boom."

Never breaking eye contact with Brock, Brandon ordered his men to case the warehouse and take any money and drugs they found. Vladimir had already retrieved the USB card that held the footage they were looking for.

With only five minutes left, all of the men exited the warehouse and hopped in Brandon's SUV that was still parked out front. They made their way down the alleyway and Vladimir and Brock exited the car and got back inside of the car they'd left at the entrance. Brandon, Zane, Devon and O'Malley turned one way and Brock and Vladimir went the opposite way.

When Brandon returned to the precinct, he briefed the Captain about the mission and reassured him that all was well again. There was no big announcement about the bust. There were no parties thrown. There was no word at all about what happened that night and that was the way Brandon and the Captain, wanted to keep it.

EPILOGUE

A few weeks later...

The word on the street was that Malik went into hiding because he had gotten in bad with some Russians and they were after him. Some people were saying that he got out of the game and moved himself and his girl to another country. Despite the rumors, only a few really knew the truth of his disappearance and neither of them intended on talking about it.

Gloria had grown terribly concerned about her son with every day that passed by. She had yet to hear from him and had been calling his phone nonstop only to get his voicemail. She began to question Brandon about his brother's whereabouts, but that was a dead end, because Brandon claimed to not know anything. He tried to reassure her that Malik was fine and that he would keep an ear to the streets and let her know if he heard anything. That helped to keep her from calling him so much and asking about Malik for awhile.

Meanwhile, Brandon spent the majority of his days combing the streets of the neighborhood and snatching up anyone who knew of or worked for his brother. He made sure that they knew what time it was and who was now in charge. Anyone who refused to adhere to the new way of things was eliminated immediately.

The rules were simple. You sell your shit and pay him a hefty fee to keep your freedom. It was that simple.

~~~~

One afternoon while Gloria was cleaning the house, she got a phone call. The phone rung several times before Gloria walked over to the wall where the phone was mounted and picked up the receiver.

"Hello?"

"Uh...um hello, Ma'am?"

"Yes."

"You don't know me, but I know your son. He gave me strict

instructions on what to do if I didn't hear from him. What I have to say to you won't be the easiest thing, but I got instructions."

Gloria's heart started to beat so fast that she thought it was going to come right out of her chest. She felt dizzy and nauseous at the same time. Her gut feeling knew exactly what was about to happen, but she didn't want to believe it. She gathered herself and calmly told the anonymous person to continue.

"I'm sorry to be the one to tell you this, but those rumors that your son ran off aren't true. Ma'am the truth is, he's dead. His pregnant girlfriend is dead too, and I was there to witness it all."

Gloria grabbed at her chest and felt weak in the knees. "Oh my God. Are you sure?" she asked.

"Yes, Ma'am. I'm sure."

Gloria held her tears in check. She needed to be strong for her son to get some answers. "Do you know who did this?"

"Unfortunately, I do."

There was a short pause on the line, but it seemed like that silence was never ending.

Nervous to hear the anonymous person's reply, Gloria swallowed the lump in her throat and asked the dreaded question. "Who was it?"

"His brother."

Gloria dropped down in the chair closest to her when her legs gave out on her. *No, no, no, no.* "Are you sure?"

"Yes Ma'am, I am. He mentioned it while they were arguing."

"Just to be sure, what was his name?" *I need to hear him say it. I need to be sure.*

"Brandon. He's a cop."

That name echoed in Gloria's ear over and over. She was hoping that this person was speaking of someone that Malik may have called his brother figuratively. That hope was shattered when the person mentioned that Brandon was a cop.

"I'm sorry Ma'am. I truly am."

Gloria dropped the phone. Her arms suddenly felt like jelly and she could feel her chest tightening. She couldn't believe that her son was gone. Her only grandbaby and possible daughter-in-law was gone as well. They were all taken away from her by the hands of her own flesh and blood.

She thought about Malik and the plans he had made to start a new life with Terry and the baby. They were going to be his reason for finally leaving that lifestyle. She would never get to witness the union between Malik and Terry and she would never get a chance to meet their unborn child.

Gloria's heart broke into a million pieces and she sat there in the chair rocking back and forth holding herself as she cried uncontrollably.

"Not my baby. I just don't understand it, Lord. Please help me to understand this," she pleaded.

Gloria cried and prayed and prayed and cried. She eventually mustered up enough strength to get herself up and go to her room. She cried herself to sleep that night the same way she did when she'd lost her husband all those years ago.

Hearing the crying on the other end, he ended the call. He thought he'd feel better letting her know the truth, but he didn't. He still felt guilty about his involvement. Killing thugs, murderers and dealers was one thing. But killing a woman was fucked up. Killing a pregnant woman was horrible and unforgiving. Although he hadn't been the one to pull the trigger, he still felt responsible because he hadn't tried to stop it.

The guilt, disappointment and shame had caused him many nights with no sleep and a few nightmares. He had put in his resignation days ago and now stood on the deck of his new house in Jamaica. He glanced over to his wife and son and knew he had made the right decision.

Nodding his head in relief, Devon walked over to join his family.

~~~~

It was a quiet Friday evening and Brandon was doing his usual patrol of the neighborhood looking for anyone he may have missed during his previous shake down. Once he realized that nothing was shaking, he started to call it a night and make his way back to the other side of town. Just as he turned his car around, his cell phone began to ring. He glanced at the screen and saw the word *Mom* and pressed the Bluetooth mode on his dashboard screen.

"Hey, Ma. Are you ok?"

"Yes. I'm fine. I wanted to see if you would be able to come and have dinner with me tonight."

Brandon smiled. Now that Malik was gone, she had been giving him more and more attention. "As a matter of fact, I sure can. I'm not too far away."

"Okay, good. The food is just about done."

"Alright. I'll see you soon."

Brandon ended the call and made a U-turn to head to his mother's house. Gloria was pulling a baked ham from the oven when Brandon walked in. Bobby Womack's, *Harry Hippie*, crooned softly from the small radio that sat on top of the countertop next to the stove.

"Ma? Are you expecting more company?" Brandon asked as he walked over and kissed her cheek.

Gloria tried not to cringe and back away from him. It was hard containing her emotions, but she kept it together and made sure not to give away any indications that she was aware of the truth regarding Malik.

"No, it's just you and me tonight son." That word left a bitter taste on her tongue. Yes, by birth Brandon was her son, but after learning about Malik's death, all the loving feelings that she felt for him as a mother died as well.

"I see you're trying to fatten me up," Brandon joked. "How do you expect me to chase down and catch criminals out there when you're feeding me like this?" He laughed and pointed at the spread of candied yams, collard greens, baked turkey wings, macaroni and cheese, cornbread muffins, mashed potatoes with gravy, upside down cake, and a pitcher of sweetened tea.

"There's enough food in here to feed a football team. What made you cook all of this?"

"Well, I was in here cleaning trying not to worry about your brother. After I did that, I got hungry and started cooking." She looked around at all the food. "I guess I went a little overboard."

Brandon's eyebrows raised as he said, "You think?"

Gloria waved him off and told him to go wash his hands while she prepared his plate. When Brandon came back to the table, he sat down ready to eat. Gloria asked him to say a prayer and afterwards they began eating their meal.

Gloria picked at her food for a bit while Brandon was devouring his like a starving man. She looked at him and felt nothing but disgust. She had been dreading this moment, but she knew it was necessary.

"So Brandon, have you gotten any new leads about where your brother could be?" She looked over at him and watched as he casually took a sip of his drink and wiped his mouth with a napkin.

"Ma, I already told you that I haven't heard anything since the last time you asked. If Malik wanted to be found, he would make it so that he could be. I'm sure he and Terry are off on some Island somewhere without a care in the world. You know how he's been talking about leaving here and starting a new life anyway." He took a bite of the ham. "Maybe he started sooner than later."

Without blinking an eye, he lied right to her face. Gloria couldn't believe how nonchalant he was about it. *Cain killed Abel*, suddenly ran through her mind. She began burning with rage on the inside, but managed to remain calm.

She looked down at her wrist watch and right on cue Brandon stopped eating and began coughing. She watched as he reached for his drink and gulped it down, then poured himself another glass. He cleared his throat and tried to take another bite of his food, but he spit it right back out when he began coughing again.

"What's the matter *son?*" The lack of emotion in her tone was instantly detected by Brandon. He had a look of confusion on his face as he made eye contact with her. Gloria folded her arms on top of the table and frowned back at him.

"What... (cough, cough). What did you do to me?"

Gloria leaned back in her seat and pulled a pack of cigarettes from the pocket of the sweater she was wearing. She removed one of the cancer sticks from the pack and placed it on the tip of her lips. She lit the cigarette, took a long drag and blew the smoke in Brandon's face making him cough even more.

Brandon's eyes bulged as he tried to catch his breath, but he was attacked with more coughs. His eyes began to water as he pulled at the neck of his shirt as if it would help to relieve his discomfort. He coughed and heaved and heaved and coughed until his nose began to bleed. He was struggling with every breath. He tried to open his mouth to say something to her, but nothing came out. Brandon continued to choke and gag on his own blood as he felt his insides burning and cramping.

"Painful isn't it? Don't worry, it will be over soon." She leaned in closer to him staring him in his face. "I know you killed my boy. I know you killed Terry and my only grandbaby. Do you remember the story of Cain and Abel?"

Brandon continued coughing and gagging. He had become

lightheaded and was starting to fade in and out. He reached for Gloria and she took his hand in hers. A weak smile touched his lips at that small touch of comfort.

"Don't fight it," she whispered as tears whelmed up in her eyes and spilled down her cheeks while she watched her youngest son dying. "You know I've prayed many nights that you would outgrow that feeling of jealousy that you had towards your brother." She shook her head as if she was remembering those nights. "I didn't want this to happen. I was hoping that you would be honest with me. I was hoping that you would be honest and tell me what you did. I tried to give you another chance at redemption and you blew it every time."

Brandon's gagging and coughing continued.

"You know, in the story about Cain and Abel, Cain killed his brother because of jealousy as well. God gave him a chance to confess what he'd done and he too lied. God's punishment for Cain was to make him live the rest of his days never forgetting the horrible thing he'd done." Gloria then released Brandon's grip from her hand. "I am not God, and I cannot ever forgive you for what you've done. Malik is no longer here, and I will never get to see him again. You took his life and now I'm taking yours."

Brandon's head lolled back as he continued trying to fight the inevitable. He gasped, coughed and choked until he finally took his last breath and succumbed to his fate. Gloria puffed on her cigarette as she stared at Brandon's lifeless body for a while, then she reached over to close his glazed over eyes. She then got up from the table and walked over to the kitchen phone. She dialed a few numbers and brought the receiver up to her ear.

"It's done," was all she said before hanging up.

Minutes later there was a knock at her door and several men dressed in dark colored clothing entered the house. They came into the kitchen and began spreading plastic out on the floor. They removed Brandon's body from the chair and placed him on top of the plastic. Two men wrapped Brandon's body in the plastic material while the other cleaned the blood from the table and the surrounding areas of the floor. No one spoke a word to Gloria. They just picked up the body and exited the house just as quickly as they'd arrived.

Gloria started to clear the table of the plates of food and the cups of tea. When she began wrapping up the left over food, she could no longer suppress her tears. Gloria cried so hard that she became too weak to hold up her own weight. She collapsed on the counter top and sobbed loudly.

Malik had been her rock throughout the years after the passing of her husband. He was the one who stepped up to help take care of them when she struggled to do so. She wasn't happy about the life he led, but she understood why he felt he had to go that route. If it weren't for Malik, they would have been homeless. Brandon would have never gone to college and she would have never been able to retire as early as she did.

Things would never be the same again. Not only was she heartbroken, but she was now alone. Although she was overwhelmed with sadness for Malik, she knew that one day soon she would hear another knock at her door. There would be two police officers standing before her to regretfully inform her that her son was dead. Despite everything else, Gloria dreaded that day the most because she didn't know if she would be able to hide her true feelings. The thought of Brandon's name left a vile taste in her mouth. However, the fact still remained that those officers were going to come and they were going to offer their condolences, but they would never know that Brandon's death was by her own hands.

-The End-

SEND MONEY ORDER/CHECK TO:	WYNN PUBLICATIONS P.O, Box 40411 2777 Brentwood RD. Raleigh, NC 27604		

NAME			
ADDRESS			
CITY			
STATE	ZIP		
EMAIL			

BOOK TITLE	PRICE EACH	QUANTITY	TOTAL
BEHIND THE MASK	12.00		
FALSE	12.00		
MY BROTHERS KEEPER PT 1	12.00		
MY BROTHERS KEEPER PT 2	12.00		

	TOTAL	
THANK YOU FOR YOUR BUSINESS	SHIPPING & HANDLING	6.00
	FINAL TOTAL	

www.ingramcontent.com/pod-product-compliance
Lightning Source LLC
Chambersburg PA
CBHW072112170626
46813CB00004B/1514